MOVIELAND

MOVIELAND

by

RAMÓN gómez de la serna

§

Translated from the
Spanish by Angel Flores

Tough Poets Press
Arlington, Massachusetts

Originally published in Spanish under the title Cinélandia.
Translated by Angel Flores.

Front cover photo of Mary Pickford c. 1920 by Nelson Evans.

Back cover photo of Ramón Gómez de la Serna, 1928.
Photographer unknown.

ISBN 978-0-578-33681-7

This edition published in 2022 by:
Tough Poets Press
Arlington, Massachusetts 02476
U.S.A.

www.toughpoets.com

ACKNOWLEDGMENTS

The translator is deeply indebted to Miss Mildred Adams for her work and interest in this version, and also to Mme. Marcelle Auclair de Prévost for many helpful suggestions.

TRANSLATOR'S NOTE

There is a man in Europe whose passport bears only his first name and no photograph. He crosses the intellectual frontiers through the sheer incantation of one word: "RAMÓN." By the acute accent on the Ó ye shall know that he is a Spaniard. An original Spaniard at that, for capitals are not supposed to be accented in Castilian. And yet the accent cannot be left out. The roundness of that accented Ó, upon which his entire name rests, is exactly like his full round healthy face. This Ó is the substitute for a photograph. His niche in the unfinished typographical cathedrals of Bibliography reads: RAMÓN gómez de la serna.

Ramón is thirty-eight years old and is the author of at least twice as many books as his years. His first volume appeared when he was fifteen. Writing is to him what breathing is to all of us. His seven fountain pens are perennially filled with red ink. Keeping them, as he does, in the upper left pocket of his coat, they probably refill themselves from the inkwell of his heart. Writing becomes something like blood-transfusion or like a continual preparation for a Wassermann test.

The history of Spanish sensibility is full of earthquakes, gargoyles and suicides. You see either the monstrous Lope de Vega running away with twenty-five hundred plays under his arm, or Goya making holy the grotesque, or Santa Teresa opening the gates of Heaven with a double key of hysteria and horse-sense. But never did the Castilian sun project the shade of a thinker writing a "Discours de la Méthode." Castile held only madmen: Don Quijote, El Greco, Unamuno—crazy heroes hunting chimeras, fighting reality, eternity, God.

And Ramón belongs to this race, to this family. Rimbaud once accepted the disorder in his mind as sacred, but Ramón has found sacred the disorder of the world. Rimbaud found his salvation by renouncing poetry, by becoming a merchant. His antiliterary attitude burned or, rather, froze him to death. Ramón, on the other hand, sets up a tent and becomes a Superclown. The world appears to him as a curiosity shop. He examines everything, seismographs every tremor, de-vertebrates every object, and, bathing it in a piscina of grace, returns it to us crowned in a diadem of smiles. His universe is atomic, and his style heaves forth sounds of breaking. The façade of old houses bathed in twilight-gray, the breasts of women, the evening stars, the chimes of ancient clocks, the shadows cast by chimneys—all that is queer and uncanny becomes the subject of his jovial autopsies, and then dances like restless motes in a musical, cindery chaos.

* * *

Ramón Gómez de la Serna was born in Madrid on July 3, 1891.

He became a lawyer so as to be able to be photographed in cap and gown, and dedicate his only picture to himself.

In 1912 he founded the Sacred Crypt of Pombo, a haven in which the most "advanced" gestures of literary Spain have been brewed.

Years ago he delivered a speech in the Alhambra, in a very solemn celebration sponsored by Manuel de Falla and Zuloaga. While he spoke, a drunken gypsy kept a gun aimed at him, and interrupted Ramón's oration from time to time with a dangerous question: "Shall I kill him now?" But the neighboring spectators advised: "Not yet!"

On another occasion he lectured on the street-lamps of Gijón. To make his words more convincing he insisted on talking from a street-lamp, but the Gijón authorities sent the police after him. And just as exciting were his lofty declamations at the Circo Madrileño (from a trapeze) and at the Cirque d'Hiver in Paris (from an elephant).

The incredible fact remains that Ramón is the only person who has visited the Prado Museum after midnight, and the only artist who keeps in his attic-tower a Madrid lamp-post, acquired after innumerable pleas and litigations from the sober Consolidated Gas Company of Madrid. The very real, genuine lamp-post bears a plate with RAMÓN in capital letters. This humble article, which has brought a strictly private street into Ramón's studio, gives the writer a healthy, midstreet, citified sensation, full of metropolitan turbulence.

* * *

Ramón has written at least half a dozen significant novels: *The Black and White Widow* (considered by the *Paris-Journal*—hurrah!—among the five greatest works of fiction of our generation), *Movieland, A Doctor of Rare Ingenuity, Torero Caracho, The Chalet of the Roses,* and *The Incongruous One;* a few original plays; some pithy essays on Goya, Poe, Picasso, Comte de Lautréamont, Oscar Wilde, Mallarmé, et al. He contributes daily to two newspapers; dozens of weekly and monthly magazines throughout the world publish his articles. But above all, Ramón has discovered a new literary genre: the *greguería,* a sort of metaphoric maxim or aphorism without any moralizing or academic heaviness. The greguerías are witty definitions, scintillating impressions and comments, facetious trivia: an ideal cocktail of haï-kaïs in prose, sauterne, Luna Park, Chamfort, roses and peppermint. . . .

Some of Ramón's work has been translated into French, German, Italian, Polish, Dutch, Russian, and I believe a few are being Japanesed. It was high time for us to have him in English. So, for the present, here is *Movieland*. . . .

Movieland deals with an ideal Hollywood, with a Hollywood more amazing, if that were possible, than the one we know. The atmosphere of Ramón's narrative reminds one of Jules Verne, of Hans Christian Andersen—only that perhaps *Movieland* is more exhilarating, more incongruous. Through Ramón's fiction one peeps into the private life of stars, attends the shooting of great films, drinks the essential *Movieland* cocktail till one becomes blissfully intoxicated with events too beautiful to be true.

ANGEL FLORES

P.S. Ramón has never been in Hollywood. Not even in the U. S. A.

CONTENTS

MOVIELAND

CHAPTER I

The Grand Burg

From the distance Movieland looks like a Constantinople combined with a little Tokio, a touch of Florence and a hint of New York. Not that all these cities are jumbled together there, but that each of its districts represents one of them.

It is like a Noah's ark of architectures. A Florentine palace, seized with that salaciousness which exotic buildings produce, looks longingly at a Grand Pagoda.

All this is in the heart of the city, in its nucleus of tall buildings. All around it the city spreads out into a thousand little square white houses, like filing cabinets with clear visages.

It is a glittering city of seashore bungalows, without a shore.

Strange panorama, looking like nothing so much as an immense Luna Park!

On nearing the city one feels as if he were seeing the collection of a great picture museum with reproductions of the buildings in all the city streets of the world. It also looks like the toy-city of the most powerful Princess in the world, the first Princess to play with a make-believe city invented just for her amusement.

The only true things are the very square little villas whose chief desire is to look like bathrooms of happiness.

To stroll through the streets of the city is like a nightmare, and the stroller becomes a circumnavigator who tours the world in an hour.

At all events, the best people of the city, its great personages, its elegant world—its men who look like sportsmen, prize fighters and tenors—meet in that part of the city which resembles New York.

In its cafés the most popular movie stars come together, all the great men of that Cinema City whose plebiscites pertain only to things of the movies.

The constitution of this city is different from the constitutions of the rest of the world. Here everything is governed by the great moving picture magnate Emerson, the film emperor.

For forty square miles around, this man with the black eyebrows and the inextirpable white beard—its roots always in sight—is the feudal lord.

Here time has a special laziness, even though people work and the best films in the world are produced.

Something of Palm Sunday morning constantly pervades the city, even on Monday nights.

And because Movieland is located in a place with the best climate in the world, the open doors and balconies emit a chatter of music—the noise of jazzbands, the lunacies of xylophones.

In the cafés it is always cocktail hour, and the bands stroll in the gardens, the violinists juggling their violins, abandoned to the jerky dance that jazz has invented.

There is much of a Deauville summer in this atmosphere—an interminable summer in a Deauville that must be at the same time a Mecca of the world.

A broad expanse of land—twenty square miles—belongs to the great moving picture firm, "The Circle."

Several cities, distinct but united, numerous gardens and little country-houses, are to be found within sixteen miles: Moorish buildings next to Scandinavian. All of it is very strange—reminiscent of those vignettes that used to illustrate old magazines, wherein cathedrals, mosques and ancient baronial manors stood side by side.

Jacques Struk, the curious young adventurer who had just

entered this city, provided with all the papers and passports and, besides, the letter of credit for twenty-five thousand dollars necessary to set one up in Movieland, watched with astonishment while this most glamorous, most eccentric of cities unfolded itself before his eyes.

Carrying his valise—in Movieland there is no one to carry other people's baggage—he was looking for a lodging.

"Will you be so kind as to tell me where there is a good hotel?" he kept asking the passers-by, but nobody noticed him.

Finally a very good-looking girl said to him:

"If you want to come home with me I'll give you lodgings. There are no hotels here as there are in other cities. There are plenty of houses for everyone and you can eat at a restaurant."

Jacques, very gratefully and with the shyness of a man who takes shelter under the umbrella of an unknown woman instead of placing her under masculine protection, walked silently by the side of his beautiful protectress who was blessed with an appetizing décolletage, which had the color and properties of vanilla ice-cream.

Many-storied houses were next to tiny ones or studios which seemed to have lowered their façades as if to permit one to see the secrets of both their souls and their structure.

Jacques was losing his head in this medley. He was bewildered by passing from Chinatown to the Ghetto, or to a Norwegian fishing village, in a few steps.

The show-windows of the stores were dazzling, effective, somewhat mystifying. Streets bore the names of the great moving picture actors who had died in the midst of their careers.

"And what is your name, miss?" asked Jacques Struk in order to break the silence of their walk.

"My name? . . . Silver Venus. . . . It's the name they have given me. On entering Movieland one loses one's name and is baptized with a screen name. . . ."

"Well, Silver Venus is very pretty," said Jacques. They were passing a city of houses with Venetian blinds when Silver Venus opened the little door of one of the stucco palaces and entered. She asked Jacques to follow her.

At first Jacques could not see the interior, it was so dark; but soon he made out a large hall around which were scattered little tables with many of those lamps, with large lampshades, so abundant in the movies. The whole formed a movie interior.

Ash-trays were skating upon all the tables. There were portraits of royalty, convincing at first sight, but on second sight it was obvious that their majesty depended only upon crowns and diadems.

Silver Venus threw her hat on an arm-chair with a movie-like gesture. Then she smoothed her hair and turned to Jacques with the assured air of one who has recovered her true self and knows her seductive coquetry to be irresistible.

"Yes, you look very cute," said Jacques.

"Let me warn you that you need only look at me for me to understand you. We have abolished words here. You can't imagine how much I hate the commonplace. . . . 'You look very cute' has already disgusted me terribly."

Jacques, as wretched as a small boy who has been scolded, took on a sad air and tightened his grip on his valise.

"I'll show you to your room. . . . Come with me."

Jacques Struk, because of that desire to wash which one feels after a journey, allowed himself to be led. He was going towards the white wash-stand that refreshes one's mind.

They ascended those stairs which are always found leading from one room to another in the movies; and he settled down in one of the luxurious chambers in which one feels the almost maternal protection of good wood.

CHAPTER II

The Land of Patent Leather Shoes

THE FALSE CITY slept all morning. No one in the streets, not a footfall on the sidewalks.

The lamplighters had forgotten to put out the street lamps and so they all tried to illumine the day—glaring wounds that gave no light, ridiculous anachronisms.

All the windows were barred by pale shutters that protected the repose of the interiors. The morning was contaminated by the butter-colored shutters turned towards the day.

Not a dog, not a peddler.

Jacques Struk had gone out too early.

Was there not a single person to explore the morning?

He saw a group of people coming toward him.

He joined them.

They were the tourists of Movieland.

The tourists moved jerkily, like flickering films.

"And that big building with the lions?"

"The Ministry of Finance of the movies. . . . There they estimate the funds that are required to produce those great films that take in fabulous sums."

The tourists stopped in front of a big building with wide windows.

"The movies' Property Room, all kinds of furniture there," the guide said, "from the primitive kind that goes to make antediluvian pictures to the latest thing. Illustrated catalogue, twenty-five dollars."

The tourists entered that immense auction room of the movies. Everything in its twenty floors was half true and half false. The black wood of the place brings on an attack of indigestion—the sort produced by eating rich chocolate.

The movies' show-cases, with hunting scenes carved on their doors, were what gave a most human, auction-room aspect to the great Property Room, cluttered up with sumptuous thrones and by medieval tabourets (those stools that one carries by inserting one's finger into a little hole).

Next they entered the Movieland Post Office. They admired the offices of the international correspondents who answered all the questions with which the world pestered them.

"Today we received a thousand letters," said the chief clerk, "asking us whether Elsa Broters is married."

The correspondence with the world's thousands of adolescents was amazing.

"Margaret Filis was born in Baltimore and she is single."

"Gracia Mora is from Cadiz and she is only sixteen."

"Edith Maguncia adores dark men."

Jacques Struk knew about this private correspondence: it had started him on the road to Movieland.

The rest of the tourists knew it also; their ardor was dimmed at the sight of innumerable letters still unopened piled on the clerks' desks.

They came out into the streets. The guide, like the subtitles in a film, passed on quickly through the streets, changing his line as he went. He headed toward the great administration building.

Pointing at it, he said:

"The palace of Director Emerson, the absolute ruler of Movieland. . . ."

Then they passed in front of the great scenic hall where interiors were shot.

It was now after one o'clock. The streets became animated

with people. It was the hour of sport-coats, white flannel trousers and polo sticks.

Every one was going toward the essential cocktail. Their stuffed-olive souls were thirsting for cocktails.

Jacques noticed that in this city everybody wore patent leather shoes, wonderful patent leather shoes, everybody—waiters, messenger-boys, everybody.

What a difference between these patent leather shoes of Movielanders and the patent leather shoes of young boarding-school boys which are like any patent leather shoes in the world!

The patent leather shoes of Movieland are versatile; instead of becoming patent leather hoofs, they become soles that adapt themselves to the world and follow its surface.

Movieland gave the impression of great wealth merely by these shining extremities, which made the city as brilliant as one of those sun-showers that fills it with optimism and Sundayness.

CHAPTER III

Elsa and Max

MAX YORK was perhaps more important in Movieland than the Director himself, for he played the principal rôles in all the big films. He was the lover of innumerable women. A conceited person, avaricious of soul, he rowed the most famous beauties on the large lake in the park.

The movies had left their impress upon him. Having worn the garb of filmland in so many pictures, he had permanently adopted the vain, overbearing manner of the frequently reëlected Congressman.

His instincts were uncurbed. In the movies strength is now passé; all one needs for success is a little cunning and a perverted sophistication.

Without sacrifice of his blond hair and his insinuating mustache, he resembled, because of his elegant thinness, an ascetic of vice.

His days were something splendid—from breakfast which he ate in the invigorating air of the beach on the small motoring table and in the company of women in bathing costumes, to the last hour of night when he supped at the small tables of the Grand Hotel with boldly, impudently decolleté women.

But today is one of those days when life is quite different from what it appears to be in novels.

On this fine afternoon with its magnificent filmland weather, Max is undecided.

"Shall I spend my siesta in Elsa's boudoir or in that of the negress with the sculptured body upon which creams shine so brightly?"

In his imagination he chose the negress.

"Her sweet voice will lull me to sleep . . . her voice makes one think of a very ripe fig that can be eaten skin and all."

But Elsa was a great star and any neglect of her might react fatally. Elsa, Movieland's queen, waited for him, frigid but tempting, like a cold jewel that fascinates its thief.

Vacillating no longer, Max jumped into his car which, as usual, throbbed in readiness below. He drove toward the suburbs, to the white châlet whose square columns typified the Movieland style of architecture.

He opened the door and entered the hall, cool with that rich shadow peculiar to those houses in which an electric cooling plant—refreshing music-box—is at work.

There were flowers in crystal vases.

Magazines, scattered here and there, lent the room cheerfulness. In some of them were displayed those female sport enthusiasts whom kodaks like to picture. On the tables radios were tuned in, for the black cobra which transforms all things into sound stands erect and proud in each Movieland home.

Women spent their evenings listening in. They were interested in nothing about them, seeking only for distant jazzbands. To be in the salon of some Grand Hotel amongst ladies who stand up continually, as if incessantly ascending, who adjust the shoulder-straps of their evening gowns for fear of being unsheathed of their chemises—that was their desire.

They longed for those distant floors upon which light searches out the cordons of dances.

They pined for those hypocritical gatherings where girls worship God with kisses enveloped in cigarette-smoke.

Max walked through rooms freshened by their morning toilette, in search of Elsa.

Elsa could be found nowhere.

He did not wish to call her; he wished to find her with dramatic finesse.

At last he cried out, "Elsa, Elsa."

There was no answer.

He cast a suspicious glance toward the closets, in which all the air of a house seemed to gather, and whose manipulation is as complicated as that needed for railway engines.

Elsa's thousand gowns rested upon the shoulders of hanged men—the clothes hangers—wide and polished.

"Elsa. Elsa."

At last Elsa appeared. She walked out of a closet.

"What were you doing in there?"

"Oh, this hot spell at the beginning of spring unnerves me, makes me ill, really kills me," she answered.

Max looked into the closet. He suspected nothing—but he looked anyhow.

"This place smells of raincoat."

"That's why I selected it. Nothing so refreshing. I fell asleep for a while and dreamed I was in a forest of umbrellas."

"You're really funny. Today you can elaborate upon the emotions of sleeping in a closet. There won't be anything left for you to try."

"To sleep in a closet is to sleep outside the world. I am quite bored with everything . . . that's why I left the earth for a while."

"Come on, silly, let's go for a ride. . . ."

Elsa stretched. She was a sumptuous woman. She was naked, as a swan is, for her white silk sheath clung to her like the swan's plumage, causing her to look naked.

Her eyes were those green eyes, so well suited for the screen—gentle, straight eyes, which offer clusters of grapes to those who watch them. Tender, bright eyes! A pretty little nose led one's eyes to the greenness of hers. One felt the glossy self-hypnotic sweetness of her pupils.

That she had been born among cactuses and palm-trees, that her mother had taught her how to curl and comb her black hair, how to give it the freshness of a well-dressed and cleansed coiffure, could easily be guessed.

Again Elsa stretched; she stood up, looked for a hat in a corner, in that corner of the world which the hands of prestidigitators always discover. She put it on nonchalantly and took a little cane.

"I'm ready."

They stepped out.

She, the motoring Amazon, knew well how to jump into the car. She sat down, looking afar, paying no attention to the machine.

The monster started going. It answered to the driving wheel as to an idea and seemed to have as much force in the rear as in front.

The enormous auto seemed to push the city away. The gust from its spurts shoved aside a few houses. It looked like an immense, motor bathroom. And they were the bathers, enjoying very cozily their ideal bath. Supine in their tub, they put out their heads, blissfully. . . .

Everything followed the rhythm of their car.

When they came to the open road they devoted themselves to speed, extracting velocity from the spirit of the car and from themselves.

Their wasted sensibilities could only be renewed through vertigo. Elsa stretched out her bare arms to speed and put on vertigo's soft, ethereal gloves.

They did not deny themselves an ounce of possible danger.

Everything was each day more permissible upon that piece of land.

And so, on this fine afternoon they felt like driving to the very kingdom of death.

The day they would reach death would be the only one devoid of monotony.

They saw the straight line that leads to the end, and they challenged it. In the speed of their car was the desire of absorbing distance, of being absorbed by it, of reaching that final destination.

The fingers of the wind frizzled and curled Elsa's hair. She received all the kisses the wind gave her.

She had the wheedling airs, the vanity and affectation of a spoiled girl nicely dolled and spruced.

She felt the contentment of a communicant leaning forward on the railing of the high-altar, avidly taking the eternal communion of the automobile.

"Max, full speed down that hill!" Elsa cried out like one asking for an excess of pleasure.

The car coasted down hill as if its mudguards had become the wings of speed. There was a moment of stripping and herring-boning in that race. One must feel just like that when the soul leaves one's body—an immaterial, hypostatic otherworldliness.

Were they dead? They looked at each other as those who return from the beyond; now the car purred along an even road.

The countryside had the aspect of a fine afternoon excellently fitted for tea-ing in the open; they felt like swallowing the entire world; such a Gargantuan meal would have been the only thing that could have satiated them.

Max drove through the pompous meadows. His excessive voracity required all the vices and all the pleasures.

If they continued speeding at such rate they would go beyond the world.

"Let's go to the village of the old hats," Elsa suggested.

The powerful driving-wheel was like the sector of an armillary sphere. It gave one the sensation that by maneuvering it one could get to unbelievable places.

A few miles from Movieland there was an old village which, on account of its tarnished and dilapidated roofs, Elsa liked to call "the village of the old hats." It remained so named forever and when autos paused by the door of some unconcerned hotel, it was frequently for the chauffeur to ask: "Is this the way to the village of old hats?"

The inhabitants of the false city were anxious to visit a real village. It was a ramshackle village full of mediocre but real people who guarded the forests and the rubber plantations of the midlands.

Descendants of explorers of history—creoles (Jews and negroes mixed)—they possessed the charm of a normal and obscure logic.

The rulers of the village prohibited its inhabitants from visiting Movieland. A permanent sign was posted on every corner stipulating fines and punishment for violators.

Max and Elsa, after contrasting their life with that of those real beings—pacific little ants—turned their car around and drove back to Movieland.

CHAPTER IV

The Villains

VILLAINS constantly arrive at Movieland.

They are corpulent, nasty, elegantly dressed. Good-for-nothings, men of no worth in their own homes; the only reasonable thing that could have been done with them, had they stayed there, would have been to exterminate them.

Since there is no place for them in real cities, these villains, loathed by society, pack bag and baggage and move to the false city.

The Director of Movieland is happy to see them.

"What a wonderful villain you make, my dear sir!" he remarks ecstatically as he observes the admirable look of complete nastiness on the face of a newcomer, a thoroughly execrable man, a king of abominations.

And the villain signs a contract proportionate to the degree of villainy he conveys.

Jacques Struk could not stand these men.

Villains who are not villains but who have atrociously villainous faces take the road to Movieland.

They have been unpleasant, repulsive, repugnant, from childhood. Everybody mistrusted them and assigned them—so detestable they looked—the worst possible rôles in life. "What a horrid face that guy has!" a fellow in the audience tells another when the-man-with-the-villainous-face stands up to observe the orchestra seats.

Because people often spied on them, the habitually scornful

and hostile expression of their faces sometimes reached a paroxysm of repellance.

An ugly twist of the mouth, a constant blank look, a strange astigmatism, a scabrous lividness of face, an appearance bold and bestial, are the characteristics of a villain.

In former times a "villain" had either to assert himself or bear a dog's life. The villain had to polish, to tune up, to profit by his malignant looks. He had to gradually conform to the type of person others wanted him to be, and content himself with frightening timid souls.

The man with the villainous face had no future. At times he would commit the crime forced on him by the unanimous petition of his neighbors' glances which were always truculently demanding that he do some terrible thing.

But to a man with a villainous face today the cinema offers a magnificent future. They take the road to Movieland, covering on foot mile after mile through devious roads so as to avoid importunate people.

Armies of villains arrive. The Director examines them.

"By God! What a criminal mug you've got there! You are employed. A thousand dollars per month."

He is so admirably perverse, so wonderfully repulsive, that his employer, charmed, begins boisterously to gather the entire company:

"Come here! Come here! What luck! Isn't he a marvellous villain."

The villain unsheaths his best expressions of malevolence, and on the screen everybody experiences a thrill of fear at the moment when, through the illuminated glass-door, he is seen observing the woman whose blood he sucks, and whose paleness increases with his cruelty.

The cinema's villains may be divided into full-dress villains and shirt-sleeve villains—gunmen or dandies.

Depraved, distrustful, elegant men, with enigmatic looks and blasphemous, revengeful mouths, receive fabulous salaries. Life, accidents and emotions are infused into the film, thanks to the wickedness of his impassible and ferocious face which without wincing defies the light from the reflectors.

VILLAINS WANTED

An ad like this attracts to Movieland those villains who make conspicuous the beauty of the women they marry in the mendacious churches of the movies—cinematographic weddings which are annulled immediately after the ceremony.

How many villains live in Movieland! They are better paid than nice, sympathetic men, and they have more privileges.

"What luck to have a villainous face," one of them told Jacques Struk. Jacques gave him a dirty look but the villain patted him affectionately on the shoulder, and insinuated:

"We're going to become pals. You are a fine fellow and my greatest desire, my greatest need, is to take refuge with a nice chap. I am so terribly repulsive!"

Such an ingenuous confession softened Jacques' heart, and he accepted the friendship of Gabriel Pontal, who so frankly admitted his nastiness.

He noticed that villains, that is to say men with a villainous face, are often fine men—good natured, resigned.

Gabriel was the fellow who in the cold, cruel films choked to death the most beautiful women.

The boundless hate produced by villains brings them together. They meet frequently. They wish to rub off their villainy against each other, to excuse themselves for their undeservedly bad reputations.

CHAPTER V

The Japanese

A GOOD JAPANESE is a most fortunate person in Movieland.

In that foreign legion of art, newcomers are never asked to show their visas. They are accepted if they do the tiger-step well and if they interpret convincingly the pantomime of rehearsal.

No one knows through what devious path a Japanese arrives in the Electric City.

It seems he has swum across the sea.

His luggage is insignificant.

His mind was made up to come to Movieland from the night he saw a film projected on a paper screen for the first time. What an immense distance separates that night from the night of his arrival in Movieland—a night illuminated by more than a thousand electric lamps!

Once he gets there, the Japanese crawls like a reptile, for fear of being caught when so near the goal—the door upon whose oval crystal one may read the word: DIRECTOR.

But he cannot see the Director as readily as he expected. Movieland's Director is much more than a Hotel Manager, who merely bosses a little office at whose door wait men in white butterfly ties aspiring to become waiters.

For three days the Jap has to wait by the directorial palace on whose flagstaff always wavers a nocturnal-blue flag with a full moon silhouetted in white upon a sky-blue background.

The Directors know that quite often these daring Japanese are fit only for playing rôles in silent words; that is why they treat them like beings of no importance.

"Have a seat," the Director orders like an Emperor. He pretends to be finishing a letter so as to observe stealthily the unknown, perhaps talented aspirant who expects to be some day the aureoled-head of great films.

After a short while, the Director tries him out:

"Are you in love?"

"Yes, sir. I love Hi-lu-la."

"Read this cable. They say she is dead."

If the Jap is clever, he gives himself up entirely to his grief and interprets it with such gestures that the Director may readily see whether he's got the goods.

"Her assassin," the Director interrupts, "is in that corner."

If the Jap is of the stuff movie-stars are made of, his expression will move even the Director, forcing him to take out his check-book hurriedly.

"There were times I had to ring the bell as if some one were being murdered in my office," declared Movieland's Director, when referring to these mock-scenes, touchstone of the cinema. "I was once moved to tears by the great Tu-Fu, who was, alas, killed by the opium he smoked in exotic films. He entered my office like that classical beggar who takes advantage of Movieland's hospitality. . . . 'Your mother is dead,' I told him. His expression was unprecedented. What childhood remembrances his face evoked! What scenes he saw from his mother's arms through the windows of his natal home!"

After the Japanese are admitted into the movies they live a silent and secluded life.

They look as though they had killed some one.

They have to be handled with care, like hot-house flowers. Thus the famous Yu-Kama is like the Emperor of Japan in Movieland.

He is the actor who during movie nights smiles dryly and

perfidiously, thrilling audiences.

His head is a lamp illuminating the evil instincts which lie within.

In the cinema, every night is Christmas Eve, when children walk around in their night-clothes. Yu-Kama and his nocturnal films frighten them.

The Japanese of the movies harm women most. With their cross looks and the oblique flight of their brows they discharge their bird-of-prey desires toward the little triangular hollow that lies in the throat of sleeping women. They endow films with an additional dimension—the dimension of their reflections—by their way of seeing the dragon and of perforating the soul's entrails.

The film becomes full of corners, and the open side of the stage is closed to the glance of the spectators. Everything then happens within closed quarters, within four walls thick with heavy tapestries, in an impenetrable and deaf room.

Japanese actors conceal their souls and do not participate in the confusion of the films. They keep their personalities nested in thin half-closed eyelids.

They distrust all that happens in the movie. By dint of their suspicion they even conceive the camera as one more character—the pragmatic eye of Providence who takes good notice of all that happens and follows the thread of vengeances and hypocrite fictions with his hands in the sleeves of his kimono.

CHAPTER VI

The City That Will Burn Tomorrow

Jacques and Silver Venus, whom he already called "Mary," seeking in her intimate name a refreshing relief from her screen alias, went out for a walk. The countryside was arid and dead as if a shower of salt had rained upon the fields.

Cinema salts had, undoubtedly, made the land sterile and nobody ever dreamed of sowing anything.

Jacques became sentimental as soon as he walked a little way from Movieland. He pressed Mary's arm caressingly. She smiled at his naïveté, with disdain.

Jacques leaned toward her, trying to inhale that perfume which dried-up, exhausted movie actresses—more than any other women—so completely lack. Jacques' infatuation increased the farther he walked from the wasteland surrounding Movieland.

"Will you always love me?"

"Where do you get that 'always' stuff from? I've never loved you!"

"But what do you call this?"

"Condescension. . . ."

"Are you afraid of loving me?"

"Yes. I hate to have to belong to one man. Free, as I am now, I can go to the country with different men. It must be a terrible bore to have to go out always with the same person."

"You are tantalizing me."

"I can't conceive how you can still talk about love after seeing the bunk we put in our films."

"I'll always suffer because of you."

"Poor fish! Love would only tie me down, but you would have to pay for it by having me hang from your neck forever. Among the young women aspiring, unsuccessfully, to become movie actresses, and with whom it is perfectly legitimate to make whoopee, there are many so pretty that at times I regret not being a man. Well then, you see, if I were to love you, they would keep away from you."

"I should worry."

"You idiot!"

They remain silent. There is something in the landscape that keeps them quiet: it is a house which bricklayers and painters are finishing up—the city that will burn tomorrow in the film *The Big Fire*.

"It's too bad that a city so carefully built is going to be destroyed," remarked Jacques.

"But we'll make a film. . . . This city will live longer than those other cities now standing up that will never be filmed!"

"Where are you to throw yourself from, Mary?"

"From the second floor."

The houses seemed to be waiting for all those whose pastime is looking for an apartment. But they were, alas, to be consumed by the flames. . . .

So that the mock city might produce the genuine emotion of a true city in flames, everything in it was real, even the window panes.

Jacques and Mary continued their walk amid the shops, which, with their fashion-plates and goods, were to burn next day. Everything contained the essential sadness of things doomed. The disappearance of the false city was mixed in their minds with the idea of their separation.

They seemed to be walking in a world similar to that whose

inhabitants dream one day of being millionaires and the next day are ruined at roulette.

Jacques was beginning to get used to the transformations that gave the city a constantly varying aspect.

The strangest thing about mock-cities is that though their street cars cover the same territory every day they seem nevertheless to be going through different cities. The repugnant monotony of a trolley line eternally reflected by the same show-windows of haberdasheries and stationery stores—show-windows filled with soap-ads and caressing shaving-brushes—could not exist in Movieland because there was a necessary and unavoidable weekly fire or demolition. All this, so amusing to Jacques, because of its novelty, only bored Mary. She hated the movies as much as any of the personages of the great cinema city.

"There can be nothing more tiresome than the movies," Mary used to say. "Managers conceal most of the suicides. The public learns only occasionally about those actors who kill themselves while on location and whose names have been divulged by some indiscreet innkeeper."

"But what's the idea of concealing news about suicides?"

"Just so that the public may not get familiar with the *materia prima* of the movies, with the stuff that inspires films. . . ."

Mary's coat, trimmed with fur, floated around her like a heavy and cumbersome bell. It was as if she were carrying a little lap-dog which, leashed to her skirt, rubbed and warmed her legs.

"You can't imagine how fond puppies are of going after these coats," she remarked in that ingenuous tone so typical of her.

They returned home. Jacques wanted Mary's kisses. He would have liked to persuade himself once more of her unbelievable beauty.

"Get rid of your animality so that your ultimate slimness may shine the more admirably." He took off her coat and became the captain of her curves.

CHAPTER VII

The Big Studio

NEAR THE BIG STUDIO stands an enormous plant which supplies the huge luminous waste of Movieland with electricity.

This ogival plant distills the thunderbolts from all the unexploited African storms.

It is the most powerful plant in the world; it was built to look like a cathedral and it is used as such for the background of many films.

The light that shines from its lofty sky-lights squints toward the moon.

The plant heaves forth a constant sound of breaking, of stopping, of fingers caught in gears, of emergency brakes put on to calm its hysteric crises.

The greatest flow from the big factory's current is consumed by the big cinematographic studio—that immense warehouse of lights, and settings, functioning now in full force.

This great granary creates general activity.

Seated before large tables, the writers of sub-titles write the captions of films with their fountain-pens of light, just as if they were the secretaries of authors. After a little experience they will begin to write luminous poems that will be great hits when inserted in films full of chlorotic lyrism.

Authors examine the ensemble, tired, perhaps from having put so many titles in circulation; yet they always consider their last effort bigger and better.

Their moviedramas and their scenarios seem to them like

catalogues of gestures which have miraculously taken form.

They feel as if they were dictating novels *to* life instead of *from* life.

The photographer is the most artisan-like of those stentorian and restless creatures.

The photographer opens and closes the diaphragm and observes the performance from the aquatic abyss of a lens. He anticipates the orders of the director who halts and rectifies the show.

The great factory of scenes is in an utter paroxysm. Movieland has become a fabulous center of super production.

From every rafter hang the fantastic spiders of chandeliers and from every corner shine clusters of lamps and a great number of those reflectors which illuminate signboards.

Samples of light, appliqué lace of light, magnificent patches of light, bring into the studio gusts of light, big plates of luminous custard.

The mercury lamps administer intramedullary injections.

Emotion takes refuge in the dark halls of the movies and in somber hearts: but here an excess of light annuls all emotions. How pitiful those creatures who, in utter incredulity, live on the wretched specter of life and its cold simulation.

Poor cinemas of the world! Roosts for the moon! Vain white sheets! Disheartening pomp! Lark hunting!

The simulation of the remote is done in terms of nearness.

One often thinks of the doorman who stands at the theater's entrance, who knows nothing and sees nothing, who has felt no one enter or leave, who hardly knows what is happening inside. As though the entire audience were to sit reading a luminous illustrated magazine. Like when, at the barber's, we open a coated paper magazine in whose glossiness we seem to see the different phases of the tonsorial operation, not only of our own, but of all those who have preceded us.

The "gagman" is seated in his corner. This cinema personage would be established in life if envy and bigotry permitted it. He seems not to do anything; he sits down quietly amid the people witnessing the shooting of the film. The author, the directors, even the actors, chat among themselves, but the "gagman" smokes his pipe and watches.

Suddenly he stands up, like a Congressman asking for the floor, and says: "Just a moment, stage-director, I believe that here we must include this or that." The performance comes to an immediate stop and everybody listens attentively to the "gagman," the official and diplomatic interruptor. His opinion is tried out and is accepted or rejected accordingly.

That's the "gagman's" sole authority. He has no excessive duties to perform, no chronometric rôle. His job does not bind him to anything—it is, therefore, an important one.

If "gagmen" were installed in real life, how willingly would many great men—who hate to collaborate in the social task because they are asked threateningly to formulate an entire program or to hatch a governmental plot—accept this rôle. Some one from a box yells what the next move is to be. . . . The "gagman" renders inestimable services!

The spectacle of life will be ample and intelligent the day when "gagmen" will be established, with a salary as generous as that of a member of Cabinet, without any fixed office hours and without too many cumbersome duties.

One can also see in the studio the prompter of expression.

This man seems hardly to exist. He runs from one corner to another, he whirls around as if dancing a difficult, bizarre and interminable rigadoon; his partner does not look at him and never gives him her hand. She always pretends to be distracted and never looks him in the eye; she is satisfied with watching herself.

Neither does the audience see this man. He never appears in

the films; he is the invisible dog, the dog that walks ahead and leads the thread of the plot.

Movieland's prompter lives half the life of the prompters of old. He is neither an actor nor a servant. He seems not to exist and yet his job remains paramount.

The main duty of the prompter of expression is to carry a looking-glass hanging from his teeth—a mercury mirror, the cleanest mirror that can be purchased at the mirror-store. The head of the actor stands out on it as if upon some luminous sky.

The expression of the movie-actor has to be attended to, has to be cared for, the actor must constantly check himself and find out how his gestures are getting along.

This looking-glass, moving, turning, butterflying, like the mirror of conscience in a symbolic drama, searches for the cinema actors and shows them the shades of their passion, of their terror, of their wrath.

Those who do not know that there is a prompter of expression with a glittering guillotining mirror, have noticed that the actors, but especially the actresses, pose and smirk lackadaisically as if in front of their dressing-table looking-glass. They realize now that such affectation springs as much from the mirror as from the conscience of the actors.

From these mirrors which follow them in their work and accompany them through the peripetiae of the drama, they sometimes extract a glance so steeped in grief that, involuntarily, they are consoled.

Their expression should nevertheless be drier and ought to be reflected in a deeper and darker abyss. The actress who would not look at herself in a mirror—it is always a mirror of coquetry—would forget herself and she would become more sincere, more intense, more lonely in the solitude of the drama.

Alas, poor, dumb, third person, obliging as an immovable wall!

The mirror becomes incrusted in the heart of the prompter of expression who carries it like a scapulary.

The mirror's profundity makes of the prompter of expression an empty, hungry man who has no business to take part in idyls, feasts or even tragedies although he moves around them, presenting his aggravating looking-glass whenever he sees that some one in a death scene is required to put on the eloquent gesture of one who is bidding farewell to himself from the last window of a train.

In the middle of the studio, at the most strategic point, stands one more authoritative than the rest: the animator.

The movies' animator is harsh as a cruel god. He has the implacable look of a magician. He is not the simple and vulgar stage-director; he is more than that: he is the creator. His position is almost as important as that of the maker of all things.

"He thinks we are dolls," the shadows of the screen say indignantly when he comes in without greeting any one, proud, ready for battle, preoccupied with the characters into whom he must infuse life.

"There's the animator," the servants say, and the movies' mannequins begin to move around, to stand up, to fix up their ties, to enlarge their decolletés, to look at themselves in their pocket-book mirrors.

The animator exacts the truth from the spectacle because for him it is the hour of creating, the hour of truth, and therefore, he lays aside whatever is not natural, vibrant, poignant.

"Pi-pi-piii. . . ."

It seems as if the animator's whistle is never going to stop, it remains pricked in the soul together with the other whistles, trains' and ferries', which one has heard and which have remained stuck in one's entrails like pins on a pin-cushion.

The animator's whistle interrupts the performance which was rushing on at full speed.

The metallic whistle, ferociously flattened as if bitten by an atrocious desire for utterance, hangs from the animator's breast like a noisy and impertinent monocle.

"Pi-pi-piii. . . ."

The trolley of the performance jumps of the tracks, gets its pole off the wire, and everybody stares as would the guests at a ball should the host begin to rave.

"Pi-pi-piii. . . ."

A couple of film sweethearts who have really fallen in love with each other during the performance continue in their ecstasy oblivious to the whistle.

"That's enough!" everybody feels like yelling—adding to "that's enough" some insulting word.

The animator's whistle then becomes a pin-prick unfelt by magnetized persons.

The animator hardly talks to the actors, he sips his cocktails silently, turning his back to the public, like a man who can't afford to be weak.

His wife is not a movie actress—he keeps her away from every one.

The animator observes life, he takes notes, calculates the amount of sincerity it contains, learns especially what is most difficult to project on the screen, something much more difficult than a passion, than a strangling, than a death rattle: the goings on of a crowd in a cabaret or on board a ship, the incurious, I-don't-give-a-damn attitude of the actors, living wrapped up in their very personal, independent, isolated, and egotistic thoughts.

As soon as the animator loses himself in one of these great problems, there is a vulgar fellow who casts a raking glance into the lens of the camera, or a woman who flirts with it, thus revealing the whole vainglorious artifice of the film.

Finally, after great exertion, the directors, tired of yelling through their megaphones, call off the show for the day.

The actresses rush toward their dressing-rooms like women who have taken a sea-bath and go in to put on their street-clothes.

They come out full of nervous tics.

They tremble with emotion after playing in emotionless dramas.

Like those women who provoke in a man a passion they themselves do not share, there throbs in these actresses a grand passion, vehement and anguished but unrequited.

"What a hit this film is going to make!" they hear directors and film-men comment.

The women have only seen the huddled side of that immense loft of the world which is a moving picture studio.

They disappear into the night of the streets.

Some of them are followed by the colorless shades of their husbands.

Their husbands are more silent than the figures on the screen, but they are useless to the cinema. They boast of being handsome without realizing that, since the hotel and the luxury belong to their wives, they are simply their butlers.

Presumptuous, imitating movie actors in their way of dressing, they are utter misfits for the celluloid pellicle.

The women are powdered with electricity. Doubtless, too much light is contagious.

The show-windows of stores shine with that excessive light of big factories, superfluous light which has to be used that same evening before it grows sour.

Movieland's jewelry shops are unparalleled, diamonds shine there better than elsewhere.

But it is in front of the silk hosiery window that women stop most frequently.

What stockings are those silk ones of Movieland!

Stockings that are frantic, criminal, stranglers of emotion, epileptic with pleasure.

Drunk with the desire of shopping, of wasting money, of pulverizing the gold they have just finished hatching in dramas, the actresses go around the stores after the great performance.

The living mannequin of the big corset shop holds their attention for a while; they watch her prepare for a voluptuous night.

As nothing of this sort is prohibited in Movieland, this extraordinary mannequin attracts the attention prodigiously: life stirs under her carnal wax and the phosphorescence of her radioactive legs filters through silk stockings.

This woman is bold. She can not smile in any definite way. The ladies become quite interested in the corset she exhibits for they see her breathing comfortably and her hips are visibly at ease.

The rumor in Movieland is that this beautiful woman is a Russian princess. Such a legend, added to her palpitating and moving beauty, compels the gentlemen to wait for her at closing time. But they are fooled because she leaves by a secret door.

CHAPTER VIII

The False Cléo De Merode

MOVIELAND WAS INTRIGUED that evening. Europe had protested against the film by a false Cléo de Merode. The woman who had personified the dancer, raising her arms indignantly, looked like a shipwrecked castaway.

The evening edition of *Filmland* summarized the whole affair.

It was read aloud by all the people around the tables:

"Women of the world, successful women, whose beauty has astonished the world, can easily be made old even by their admirers, piling on them a few extra years.

"Cléo de Merode has experienced the consequences of publicity and success, but she is still beautiful, her profile is made of a material less fragile than that of other women.

"Just now she has started suit against a moving-picture concern that has been exhibiting in Paris a film which came from Movieland where it was produced under the title: 'Cléo, the great Parisian dancer, her love-affairs, her private life.'"

Cléo de Merode complained of the similarity in name and, with the agility of a woman of the world, went to court wrapped in a sumptuous fur coat, her car full of flowers and cushions. She brought along her lawyer, Mr. Valensi.

Cléo has always been, in the eyes of the public, the immaculate beauty. Her name may be in everybody's mouth but this talk never goes beyond trivial gossip. She attacked this film especially because its heroine does not live an exemplary life: she gets drunk and removes her clothing in a cabaret, in the company of debilitated old film men.

"I went to see myself in that film and I cried with shame and indignation," she told the Judge furiously. "If at least the heroine were as beautiful as I am . . . but she is a poor fool," she went on, "who resembles me only in the way she combs her hair, covering her ears with the waves that characterize me."

The Judge heard her with the utmost politeness and ordered the film to be suppressed.

Cléo de Merode, woman extraordinary, whom people suspected not to have any ears, and whose picture appeared in all match-boxes, the woman with the poetic face of an ideal queen of floral games, in whose honor people called the King of Belgium "Cléopold" instead of Leopold, has thus saved her prestige and expects now to collect a heavy indemnity.

Every one sympathizes with this mysterious woman who, covering her ears with her curls so as not to listen to the rabble's flatteries, walks by, hermetic and unsullied, as if encased in a jewel box. Why should she wear earrings? Why should she carry on her savage lobes two huge pearls, she who is a pearl herself?

We can all recall in our lives a woman, with her hair dressed *à la Cléo Merode,* a dreamy girl with the long scroll of romance in her hands. Cléo de Merode as the impersonation of romanticism, of the woman who with abstracted glances divests herself of a trailing gown, of an adorable creature who may have written us on stationery that has a swallow for a letterhead.

Languid Cléo de Merode, who might have been named after a courtesan of antiquity or a succulent fairy, could not bear the breath of slander. She is so clean, so beautiful, so brilliant, that sin has never soiled her; she is less soiled than women who never sin; her long white kid gloves (covering her vaccination marks) have always remained spotless, without those stains which small change always leaves on the gloves of bourgeois maidens.

"To dare say that I am less beautiful than Cléo, when I have actually improved on her!" the false Cléo was saying, perched on the highest stool of the bar.

"At least I have ears," she went on, showing the pearly shells of her tiny ears.

"You are really more Cléo de Merode than she is herself. She is a Cléo unconsciously but you are a conscious Cléo. You are more aware of what is needed to make a Cléo de Merode," said Wilh, who had approached her that evening to drink the champagne of notoriety.

CHAPTER IX

The Gloomy Men

In Movieland there are men who look neither wicked nor Chinese, neither do they bite their lips.

These men are men with somber faculties. They darken the room as they enter. Seated at a corner in a movie tavern, they fill it with a sullen magic.

Perhaps it is because they do not utter a single word, because they speak to no one; they just smoke their own pipes by themselves, but, nevertheless, they create an atmosphere, localize it as do these lamps, gnats of light which begin to dance at the hour of chair-throwing riots.

These men were born gloomy and their destiny is as dark as a black-light lamp.

In Movieland they are so immersed in their dark dreams that they have become inoffensive.

Their lives flow like black waters in expensive drains.

Sharing the general excuse found by every one sitting on Movieland's terraces to enjoy himself, the gloomy men look tranquil.

"Who is that chap?" asks the inexperienced new arrival at Movieland.

"He is a 'gloomy man,'" the guide answers immediately, and such a title permits the gloomy man in question to remain placidly seated on his wicker chair. On seeing himself watched by some one, he smokes his pipe faster and puffs out a double mouthful of smoke.

Gloomy men offer such a contrast to the life of Movieland that whenever a big party is organized people always remember to have one of them present.

"We must invite a gloomy man," the hostess remarks, as if the menu cannot be complete without these dark mollusks.

The gloomy men live blissfully immersed in their happy gloominess and they are the ones who most frequently appear on Movieland's balconies, watching, for many afternoons, the spectral Montgolfiers of their smoke ascend.

The gloomy men have their love-affairs too, but they select their women carefully. The chosen ones are ladies who are lugubriously hoarse, with a huskiness that makes the day sullen, a hoarseness so clamped to the throat that no lozenge could possibly relieve it.

The gloomy men are those somber gusts of wind that must be brought, for contrast's sake, to cities which like Movieland are entirely too clear and too happy.

The President of these men, for the gloomy men form a division of the Actors' Guild, is Montenegro, a Spaniard born in Jaca and since childhood possessed by evil spirits.

Montenegro bears his supreme gloominess with solemn elegance and when a picture requires a mysterious hand to sic the spiders of terror onto the spectators' nerves, it is always Montenegro who projects his hand upon the white paper of the cinema.

The creature whose shadow haunts walls is Montenegro, always Montenegro. He tightens his belt before entering into action . . . the secret of a redoubtable, awe-inspiring silhouette involving wide shoulders and a thin waist, constricted like those of negro idols.

Montenegro is the only gloomy man who does not care for gloomy women; he loves those white, perfumed women who make excellent ads for the movies' great toothpaste. They follow him like big white hounds, wearing tight silks upon the slippery and tender cheeks of their graceful arses.

CHAPTER X

The Bored One

THE MOST CONSPICUOUS woman in Movieland—she who flutters most around the streets, leaving in her wake the desperate flight of her coat—is the bored one.

A weary night-lamp shines in her sad eyes.

To her Movieland is a city where everything has been paid for—a city spent, without amusement.

The evenings seem to her interminable and she is nauseated with the cinemas, filled with her monotonous beauty.

When she is not at a wild party, when no one invites her out, when she has no appointments, she endeavors to lull to sleep her cruelty—that cruelty which makes her yell like a priestess of Bacchanals. She loses her slippers and her diamonds, she gives away her pocketbook with all her money to the driver who brings her home.

Silence gets on her nerves, she can't stand it—not that it is so full of remorse or of reproaches but because it is full of nothing, because its solitary snowflakes fall one by one into her lonely chamber.

Those evenings when no one rings her bell, when automobiles—whose closed hoods are dominoes and whose slits are the eyes of masks—do not hum at her door, she takes refuge in an artificial paradise; voluptuousness fills her veins, and her heart, falling asleep in turn, begins to dream.

This fatal woman loves the emotions produced by shattering glass, by the breaking of the stems of goblets, by the wolfish cries from stewed young men and by the melancholy faces of sentimental fools frightened by such a spectacle. She pushes her friends from the restaurant into the gambling-room and there amuses herself malignantly.

On tiresome days when all her friends are in bed with the flu or have gone to a family reunion, she feels lonesome, lies on her chaise-longue "like a patient etherized upon a table" and lets forbidden pleasures desiccate her.

Does she behold marvellous spectacles? Perhaps she does, but nothing can compare to the day when she will suppress the future, when she will die young. . . .

Forgotten in her boudoirs of boredom, incapable of committing suicide, the vicious woman dies little by little. If she were to fall into death's bloody cistern, how she would cling to its walls, how she would scratch them trying to get out! . . .

She was doomed, she was gradually dying, when the young, optimistic Dr. Percent made up his mind to save her.

Dr. Percent, who was in love with her, was determined to save her from cocaine. Just as a friend protects a woman who has taken refuge in his house by pointing out from the balcony the apache who awaits in the street to kill her, Dr. Percent sequestered her.

Day and night the apache cocaine walked up and down the street where the object of his desires had been imprisoned. The young doctor watched over her and bolted all the doors so that the enemy could not carry away the lovely captive.

She was suffering but she begged the doctor: "For God's sake don't leave me alone! Save me!"

A struggle went on in her mind similar to those that once took place in the cages of history between a lion and a bull or a tiger and an elephant.

At times the doctor found his fair suicide desperate because she could not survive without her cocaine; but on other occasions she triumphantly reorganized her life without drugs.

The doctor worked cautiously against cocaine, banishing it from her heart, administering instead unwholesome caresses which brought to mind the abject lover.

One night, Dr. Percent found a dose of cocaine in the electric pear attached to her bed-lamp. He scolded her severely. Pale and furious, seeing that she was going to lose delights so ingeniously concealed, she jumped at Dr. Percent's neck and bit him to death.

She then summoned all her servants and gave herself up to that inundating crisis of tears, so typical of dope-fiends and occasional criminals.

Will Movieland's justice be too harsh toward the woman conquered by the tiger of cocaine?

CHAPTER XI

The Stolen Beauty Spot

A FEW DAYS LATER another tragic event held Movieland's attention. To the door of the big studio was affixed the following notice: "Work has been suspended due to the illness of Edna Blake."

The thought of what had actually happened gave everybody the fidgets: to tear out a palpitating beauty spot is like extricating an eye, like brutally extracting a dark thought from the flesh of a living, rough, unpolished ruby.

Edna Blake's husband, her persecutor in the films—the cinema had successfully taken advantage of and capitalized the genuine hatred of this deceived husband—had bound her and cut out with a bistoury the magnificent beauty spot that enhanced her back. Ernest Word had dug down so deep, in tearing it out, that he had opened a blood-vessel through which Edna nearly bled to death, as if the beauty spot had been the cork stopping all her blood.

The daily *Filmland* published the details of the crime:

> Ernest Word cynically confessed to his eradication of that beauty spot which, he claimed, caused his wife to be unfaithful.
>
> "I wanted to tear it out roots and all so that it will never grow again; that's why I dug so deep. . . ."
>
> Edna Blake uttered only one word: "Thief," but it was pronounced in a most pitiable pathetic tone. She didn't call him a criminal. To her the cutting of the beauty spot

had been just downright robbery, a theft amounting to several million dollars. Not the biggest diamond set in platinum could repay for her beauty spot.

"Paint one on," friends counselled her but she replied disconsolately:

"I could do that, but what's the use? . . . Every one will know that it's just a makeup."

A few days before the incident, Edna's husband told Mac Porlan:

"When a woman carries her wickedness on her back or on the corners of her shoulders, there's nothing to be done about it; my wife's perversity emanates from the beauty spot on her back."

"But a beauty spot can't possibly influence her mind. You talk about it as if it were the worm of evil," Mac answered.

"She has turned her back on herself and thinks that her beauty spot shines more brilliantly than any beacon."

The Director will probably have Ernest Word exiled, and annul the marriage.

Reporters made known other actors' opinions about Ernest's deed:

Jacques Struk said that the only decent thing to do, under the circumstances, was to give the beauty spot back to Edna. "A beauty spot should be torn out of the thief and incrusted on Edna's back. If he has none one can be fashioned from a piece of his flesh by burning it in slow fire to the precise nuance of Edna's beauty spot."

Elsa said: "If a man were to do that to me, I'd bite off his nose."

"This cannibal should be deported to the Hottentots. . . . If he only knew how many charming beauty spots I have, he would swallow me up," commented the unspotted Mary.

Men were more benevolent. Max York said: "He has acted like

a fool. A beauty spot is a delicious mouthful to be swallowed like an oyster, without using a fork or a knife. Ernest Word is frightfully ignorant of the niceties of table manners."

Director Emerson said: "It's not only an infamy but a swindle—he has ruined our best trade mark. For that alone he'll be fired and he will have to pay $50,000 to boot."

Beauty spots became the topic of conversation in all the bars. When tipplers stirred with their straws and teaspoons the sediment of drinks, as if trying to dissolve something, it was, doubtless, Edna's beauty spot which they tried to mix with the last draught in their tumblers. The price of women with beauty spots went up because every man, obsessed by the idea, wanted to observe the palpable nature of beauty spots.

"What a pity!" the best writer of cheap scenarios remarked from his high bar-stool. "If they had only warned us, we might have shot the best film of the season then and there. And what a peach of a title: *The Stolen Beauty Spot!*"

Even the moon of that splendid night had a coquettish beauty spot punctuating the corners of its wide smile.

The trees lifted their heads toward the seductive moon and the inactive reflectors of the cinema were focussed upon that strange, fascinating, parodic moon, inconceivable on any sky but Movieland's.

CHAPTER XII

Absurd Cocktails

The principal bar in Movieland, the cheerful city of eternal week-ends, has high stools to which one must ascend with a ladder. The toper resembles the look-out man on the summit of his tower.

The queerest fellows get together in this bar and their conversation glitters like so many monocles.

But let's forget the chaps, with whom we are somewhat acquainted, and examine, instead, the cocktails they drink.

The cocktails imbibed in Movieland are terrible, like turpentine mixed with alcohols extracted from precious woods.

When served in tall glasses they look like stockings with varicolored stripes or like elongated purses made with polychrome beads. They hiss and crackle in the stomach like furious fireworks, causing varied degrees of ravage.

Some of them become striped panthers and it is appalling to see them coasting down the throat.

"What a swell cocktail you're drinking today!" a cinema lady tells a monopolizer of the delights.

Magnificent eggs laid by plump hens in the cinematographic poultry yard lend the glasses their yolks of melted sun and condensed morning.

The expert waiters trained in studio cafés seize the bottles by their necks, in clusters, to concoct the preparation ordered. They recognize the bottles on the shelves with a twinkle of their cocktail eyes and the bottles, clashing against each other, produce varied xylophonic impromptus.

"Give me an Antilles cocktail."

"And a Prairy cocktail for me."

"And for me a Charlot."

After a Charlot cocktail one imitates, whether one wants to or not, Charlie Chaplin; one is swayed by a fatally Chaplinesque Saint Vitus' dance, and with a little crooked cane one begins to hook the passer-by's neck, legs or arms.

"Waiter, a Mary Pickford cocktail."

This cocktail produces in one's soul the same effect as the provoking grace of its namesake. One begins from then on to live the mad existence of a love-at-first-sight lover and goes after the pretty actress' well manicured and very holy hand.

But quite often the composition of certain cocktails is never determined and the waiter scribbles, like a hurried reporter, a fantastic formula on an extremely long pad of paper:

"A glass of gin, (almost all cocktails begin the same way) a tablespoon of curaçao, a glass of vermouth Torino, a glass of whisky, two tablespoons of Alkermes, five drops of bitters, and a cherry for ornament. . . ."

It was like a prescription with the thirsty person's instruction "To be filled immediately" appended to it. Sometimes the flower from a lady's hat was used to ornament a cocktail.

Everybody in Movieland still recalls the great actor who used to play the rôle of a consumptive man in the films and how he drank a suicide cocktail which took a great deal of his time and talent to concoct. Every one saw him preparing the long poem of his ultimate cocktail till the day arrived when he climbed upon his stool, as one climbs to paradise. He handed the empty glass back to a waiter in a white jacket. Every one awaited impatiently for results looking up as if the consumptive actor had been one of those acrobats who walk on the cornices of skyscrapers, tickling thus the loins of Providence. Soon enough they saw the end: the pale man, caressing his long sea-weed beard, which seemed to have been grown under stagnant water, smiled and like an aviator, fell down dead under his stool.

No one has ever again tried out that suicidal formula; it's the only alchemy prohibited in Movieland's principal bar, though every one is slowly committing suicide. Movie actors reel out the film of their own lives, shortening it now and then so as to make a perfect picture. They do not forget the good old cinema proverb to the effect that ten thousand feet of film must be wasted to get three thousand good ones. How they waste celluloid in trying to abridge their lives! . . .

Magnificent bar where one can drink the ideal cocktail!

"I'll take one now that will make my heart dance a tango," says a great actress, from a private booth inside.

"Mine makes my heart dance a Viennese waltz," answers her companion, whose cocktail, of sober composition, resembles a jar of brilliantine at rest.

"Well, my heart goes in for Russian ballets," remarks a fellow with the face of a bankrupt gambler, sitting at a neighboring table; his gray hair possesses that chalky whiteness so typical of gamblers who should have committed suicide but who didn't have the nerve.

"I prefer vodka and kûmmel," says an eccentric beauty.

"My heart is beginning to dance the black-bottom," declares a negro in a jazzy voice.

And the deceitful cocktails—which conceal their alcohol under the guise of nourishment, since they are prepared like the sauces of great chefs accompanied by a terrific culinary din—are poured profusely every day in Movieland's principal bar to excite all those who have concluded that they are becoming ghosts and are driven to despair on that account.

CHAPTER XIII

Broken Credulity

SCEPTICISM FLOATS on the surface of Movieland.

Here things happen as they will some day happen in the rest of the world when there will be no more proletarians.

People do their thinking as if from tree-tops, oblivious of the social machinery.

Sweet, miraculous breezes cool their foreheads like the doctor's antiseptic gauzes.

Movielanders are libertines enjoying an eternal Sabbath, caring only to preserve the agility of their movements and their frank spontaneity.

They all wear new suits and no trousers bag. They are happy and unprejudiced; they are not afraid of each other.

They possess an unmistakable intuition about things in general and this makes them cheerful. They have represented ancient times under modern skies and they have come to realize the immense lies inherent in both the ancient and the modern. In the course of an afternoon they can witness the humbug of history.

They all go to a sham business, strolling on sidewalks in a perpetual tourists' town.

They are the spoiled children of a city in which it is always permissible to loaf around; they walk in file, one after another, in the expectation of adding to their lives a few musical notes.

In Movieland no one takes himself seriously.

The sober gentleman who wears an old derby full of old

ideas—a bee hive of tradition—is not to be found, thank God, in Movieland.

The tap-tap from the canes of gentlemen who stroll parsimoniously in all great cities, is not to be heard in Movieland.

The lady loaded with children whom she believes to be Little Lord Fauntleroys is not to be seen in Movieland.

But the procession of beauties is interminable.

They are aloof beauties, beyond photography, inaccessible to kodaks—charming beauties made of cinema flesh, full of cinema dimples.

Even when inspected at close quarters they keep a vague remoteness and a sensual freshness, as irritating as that of a recent corpse seen through the glass of the coffin.

Movie physicians are the only persons who invest Movieland with a little seriousness.

Movieland is full of false physicians. . . . When some one asks: "Who is that bird?" and the reply is: "Why, Dr. So and So. . . ," one should not take it too seriously. Movieland's physicians are generally false physicians who look like eminent doctors and whose presence makes us feel surer of life.

False physicians are much welcomed in Movieland's parties and banquets.

The false physicians, whose flashing spectacles shine over their brown beards, walk solemnly through streets crowded with newly married couples who delight in the bonbons of their honeymoon.

But like all men wearing medical beards they stammer amorous words confusedly, bite their beards, and stifle in them as soon as they begin to play at love.

Inconceivable Movieland crowds!

These vagabonds of the world, so devoted to wild parties, are inevitably melancholy.

They can not elude the maladies that the day suffers all over the world. Especially in the evening, Movieland anguishes with the same pain that at twilight all the cities in the world experience—cities that then become mangled, rent, decadent.

"Is it possible that this cruel pain touches *even* Movieland?" everybody asks himself, surprised on seeing that a pestering wind fans even a city without hard or severe duties.

The evening crushes the water lilies on the tranquil lake.

The day is wounded in the loins and everybody feels the pain in his own left side.

And how about death? Does not death worry them at all?

Sometimes. But they know how to conceal it so well!

Though in Movieland it is quite permissible to die, it is strictly forbidden to get in touch with dying people; they are carried to big white hospitals, and if they die on the way, in a busy avenue, it is seen to that no one becomes aware of the fact.

Funerals are performed in great secrecy. Corpses are taken away in milk-wagons, in moving vans. . . .

"What has become of So and So?" some one asks. "Why, he's gone away and left no address,"—such is the ritual answer discreetly announcing the death of some Movielander.

Now and then the friends of one of those who go away without leaving an address get together to commemorate the deceased's anniversary. They come out from these feasts drunk with tears, for their drunkenness had to be, this time at least, lugubrious.

Movieland's physicians are light-hearted and playful; their mission is to cure their patients or to *precipitate* their end by means of a gay, extravagant and exhilarating treatment.

CHAPTER XIV

The Last Word in Fairs

THE BOOTHS THAT ATTRACT Movieland's crowds most are those displaying such lively signs as: "Naked mad women," "Tattooed breasts," "Colored women in their first day of puberty," etc., etc.

Movieland has a permanent fair-ground in which the world's latest novelties are exhibited.

Things prohibited everywhere else are exhibited in Movieland. The great exposition-hall resembles a well-illuminated and immense studio.

Here original and monstrous things are assembled.

Threadless knitted gowns and electric bracelets are sold at a counter. Strewn everywhere are piles of fantastic pamphlets.

On a huge stand is displayed an automobile that flies, swims and runs.

Farther on a big electric sign reads:

PHOTOGENIC STOCKINGS

The silk of these marvellous stockings shines, titillates and tickles the air surcharged with cinema-waves.

Some women dressed in petticoats which barely cover their thighs read, sew or take tea, but always exhibit their photogenic stockings, the "knock-out" stockings which camera lenses love so well and which, when photographed, shine like fireflies.

A signboard, akin to the "Please do not touch" variety, proclaims most temptingly:

YOU CAN TOUCH THE LEGS

Inquisitive men in the crowd start conversation with the stockinged mannequins and touch their legs voluptuously.

The women who wear stockings which make well-shaped legs glitter viciously and curl the caresses of the air about them easily become man-traps.

One can hear the spurs of femininity sound whenever the photogenic-stockinged mannequins move around.

"At our feet! At our feet!" their glances say.

A little farther a placard reads:

EUGENIC PRODUCTS

Once upon a time, the eugenic theory was very much in vogue. Many have forgotten all about it but sixteen years ago it used to be a serious topic of conversation. Mlle. Marion de Pic is now sixteen years old and she is exhibited in a glass case at Movieland's exposition. Mlle. de Pic is a beautiful, sumptuous and majestic girl. Her height corresponds to her weight and her weight to her height. She is dressed in transparent robes so that every one may admire her marvellous shape—and she is really ravishing.

Her grandfather, who allowed his robust daughter, Christina Ronceau, to marry Maximilianus Ross, the handsomest lad from New-Staat, is now selling a book on Eugenics, at the same stand where the product of this perfect union is exhibited.

His book contains the entire history of the case. Mr. Ronceau had, from behind a curtain, observed every phase of this union consecrated by all the principles and laws of science.

"Before giving my daughter to my son-in-law, I took him to a doctor who punctured his spinal bulb and extracted his cephalo-spinal liquid.

"Though I knew his parents, I asked them, nevertheless, the

most intimate questions. I was helped in my researches by Dr. Sewenson, of the Academy of Sciences. The distinguished savant raised a million dollars to defray part of the expenses. I then gave the boy my robust daughter, a perfectly healthy creature, daughter and granddaughter of parents who die only of old age, after their ninetieth birthday."

The people who sit down on the divans to read the monograph about this one-woman show, which might be compared to the only statue of a supreme sculptor, raise their eyes, now and then, to illustrate their reading with a view of the wonderful Amazon who when she crosses her legs shows the most beautiful columns in the world.

The eugenic girl is like the princess of the story who was willing to take any adventurer for her love provided he fulfilled the required conditions: at the end of the Fair she will marry the man worthy of her hand. A jury composed of physicians will decide the case.

This example of positive eugenics reminds one of Sparta, where weaklings were thrown down an abyss.

The beautiful girl is a charming specimen of a eugenic female.

Movieland's public likes to examine her closely and first-row orchestra seats are quoted at impossible prices.

That woman will remain imperishably in men's memory as the supreme personification of all that is perfect, harmonious and sweet in life.

Under the moth-eaten roof of the Fair's great pavilion there is a blue booth with the sign:

WOMAN AND HER MAN
A UNIQUE PHENOMENON

Crowds went in to see that.

Half naked, a man and a woman, their bodies segmented into

one trunk, tried to separate, to get away from each other, tearing their flesh like a banana stripped from the raceme or like two bananas united by a teratological accident.

This was the perfect couple, as our jealous egos might have conceived it. Constrained by an absolute fidelity, they were sated with fidelity. Human nature requires a prudent and cautious infidelity.

One came out from that blue booth, depressed by the sadness of a bond that could not be broken, for, according to the prospectus, separation meant death: "They will die together because their bronchial tubes are engrafted at the insertion center."

The plants at the Fair are remarkable—both grotesque and rare, some of them costing as much as two or three thousand dollars a piece.

The section devoted to dogs is also extraordinary with its ridiculous puppies: some made, as it were, from a living, mobile and hopping lava; others resembling down wound into little balls; and still others born from those hairs that women gather from their combs and throw every morning out of all the windows in the world.

Farther on, one comes to an artificial lake in which swans and women swim together. The sign on the colonnade reads:

SURPLUS BATHERS

Beautiful women, whose nudity is accentuated by their bathing-costumes, stand by columns wonderfully suited for whipping posts at which women are flagellated.

The bathers offer themselves publicly for they can not earn a living in their bathing racket, especially since baths are so enervating.

Bold, gay actors take them away, holding their arms laughingly, as if they were bringing home a sponge for their ablutions or an essential and most perfect hygienic utensil which well regulated households must have.

Things such as the above were rented, sold or gratuitously given away at the free Fair of Movieland.

CHAPTER XV

Mary's Idyl

IN SPITE OF HER MOODS, her despondency and her innocent gaze, Mary was the most shameless of women.

She didn't know how to wait. She would give herself up as water gives itself to the thirsty person.

But immediately afterward she recovered her moodiness and her despondency, lifting her eyes most wistfully.

She was the ingenue of the cinema, the young lady dressed in white who personifies innocence in gardens bathed in sunshine, spangled with leaves.

In the films Mary appeared under the shrubs nervously tearing a branch, forever listening to words of love murmured by some wooer or other.

After such scenes in which she was the pure and radiant butterfly of the garden, she would begin once more to exhibit everywhere the wide step-ins she was wearing.

"For God's sake, Mary!" Jacques used to tell her, entirely at a loss. No use of talking. Mary went on with her auto-rides.

"I love it most," she said, "when the chauffeur unsheathes the sword of his speed."

How sagacious Mary was! She excited everybody in every way at all hours of the day—in the morning, in the afternoon, at night.

She imperiled the moral illusion of the cinema more than any other actress; she always played the rôle of a movie virgin, of an innocent victim, of the queen of naïveté.

Jacques suffered, seduced by this mixture of folly and horse-sense.

Their conversations were depressing. With an egotism which was reflected in all mirrors, Jacques wanted Mary to be a more faithful creature.

"The movies have exhausted me," Mary said. "My last sediment of love, which I was forced to adumbrate in my latest pictures, dates back to a period when I was playing in film No. 1000. But after that. . . !"

Beautiful, pale, deaf in all her pores, the famous actress could no longer feel the thrill of love.

She offered herself to all her admirers with that inscription on her photos which was not inscribed perhaps, but printed.

She suffered from that cinema paralysis which permits the patient to assume innumerable attitudes.

Her beauty was polished, adorned and smelled of new skin as if she had just come out from the factory.

She was afraid of Jacques because she found in him the hostile sweetheart who liked to criticize the expression which was making her famous—an expression of debutante coquetry, a subway platform expression, a boat-coming-alongside-the-pier expression.

That Ritzy, high-hattish mannerism which certain impecunious young ladies take and which sorely irritates their romantic sweethearts, now triumphed in Mary and made her really Ritzy.

She stood Jacques' nastiness and even then had charming words for him.

"If I didn't have my picture taken for you alone, do you think I would come out so well?"

"Don't fib now, your photos are for every Tom, Dick, and Harry. . . ."

"That's not so. . . . If that were the case then I should look indifferent and haughty. My pictures are taken for you and that's why they are so passionately intense."

"I see, then your little love is not entirely disinterested, there's a good reason for it. . . ."

"You scoundrel! Who ever thinks about interest when having one's picture taken?"

"You're success hungry and you take advantage of every opportunity to make a hit. . . ."

Jacques tried to be tender, but soon enough he reverted to his cruel analysis.

"The soul is cremated while the film is being shot," he remarked.

"Well, what about it? It's nice not to have a soul," she replied with ill-becoming cynicism. "This suppression of the soul is not more universal for the simple reason that few people know how to get rid of their souls. A soulless world would be a rather decent place to live in. . . ."

Their discussion became painful. Jacques, a stranger in Movieland, could not adapt himself to the milieu.

Mary confessed sometimes too sincerely:

"I have slipped up on myself. I don't know whether I am a heroine from the Middle Ages or a modern woman. I wear long train gowns and shockingly short skirts at one and the same time."

"That's all literature!"

"Not even that. . . . It's only confusion, coldness. My sole consolations are shopping and speed."

Jacques, a man from the old world, did not approve of her way of living and struggled violently with himself.

He could not adjust himself. He loved this woman too much. He saw her arms thrown around the entire world of men and the play-boys of the world stealing the breasts from her décolletage, taking away the innumerable breasts from her petticoat bodice.

CHAPTER XVI

The Museum of Expression

JUST AS ONE FINDS in Movieland the finest hospital in the world, with its nickel trimmings gleaming brilliantly, so one finds an insane asylum resembling a magnificent hotel: with dining-rooms dotted with cozy tables, with luxurious bathrooms and showers, gymnasiums, libraries and ballrooms.

Pictures concerning the insane are so perfect when filmed in Movieland because their actors are old stars who have gone mad in the midst of strange and dangerous adventures.

To avoid calling this establishment "Insane Asylum"—a name which certainly would have terrified and irritated Movieland—it has been dubbed:

MUSEUM OF EXPRESSION

This is the only sad establishment in Movieland—the only one, because even the hospital is full of entertaining things.

Movieland's insane asylum is crowded with those actors who have remained in their cinematic rôles. Poor weaklings who, one silent night, believed in all the lies of a scenario; pitiful creatures who believe in a world so artificially conceived that they really thought that they had been transported to a different time and space, to another planet.

These lunatics attained the most fantastic spasms of expression. Of original expressions, each had but one—one, however, which has remained fixed, immovable, opening on an abyss.

Their dumb expression went beyond its usual dimension, disorbed, as if in utter and definitive insanity there was room for both talented lunatics and common lunatics.

Madmen attach themselves to their world and cling so well to their rôles that their masks seem carved of the rough stone of space.

They resemble the cuttings from a film, the dried pinkings of a cinema show. Nightmares have that same queer movement felt in a roll of film constantly unrolling, in a skein unwinding itself, in soldiers marking time but not advancing, walking long distances on the same spot.

These madmen possessed luminous expressions as though the projector still shone upon them, and together they all looked like films interrupted in the midst of expressing fifty different emotions.

There might be found the celebrated Ericson who had gained world-wide recognition as the human monkey, by his manner of climbing trees, by his extraordinary simian grace.

There, also, is Alexander Barold, the queer fellow who could make an audience shudder by his manner of glancing about a room when looking for some one.

The Japanese Hin-Chey who had a frozen look of horror, as if all the dragons had been conjured against him.

As for women, the "Museum" included the queerest specimens of females in blissful ecstasies or uncontrollable rages, with contumaciously vacant eyes.

Ravishingly beautiful women lived forever in the most unbelievable of their expressions—pensive, tearful, loving.

Some mourned a love which would never return, whose passing they did not understand, whose existence they even doubted. One wonders if they went insane from having exaggerated the expressions they were told to register in an emotional crisis.

But these women are as mad as raving maniacs. Projecting

machines always flood the screens with the sunlight of their madness.

Their immense eyelids which give a satin gloss to their eyes cast languorous glances, like lids bleeding tears.

Insane-asylum angels occasionally fly into this women's prison. They are provoking angels who do not care to conceal their genitals—rosy, tender, elephantine angels who, since God takes care of all living creatures, arouse the lunatic women in their solitude.

Among the mad actresses, how many Francesca Bertinis, unable to go beyond their one eternal pose! How many Menichellis whose long, naked arms might have put handles on esthetics! How many Mary Pickfords full of that ingenuousness which does not see, nor understand, with their suit cases always at hand, on the eternal platform of the movies!

The white effusion of their insanity, of their ecstasy, is contagious: the trees in the orchard become insane; the sensual trees, tattooed by insanity, make incomprehensible confessions.

It seems that all these lunatic women dream of their films, projected somewhere, far, far away—films in which they lived another life, when they still were able to come out of their only expression, when they were able to ride along many roads in the cars of insanity, receiving full in their faces the vitriol of speed.

Their breasts are not insane yet no one caresses them now, except those fast, hernial, degenerate angels who pet them and occasionally caress them to death.

CHAPTER XVII

The Luminous Woman

MOVIELAND'S GREAT FESTIVAL coincides with the joyous moon of May.

On the first night of the full moon suppers served in the moonlight become an orgy in which the shadows of cinematography, made of lampblack and moonwhite, seek the demonstration of their reality.

The "movielanguid" moon projects upon her round screen passionate scenes in which men become humid earthworms.

The fields smell of banks of frogs terrified by the resurrection of ancient shadows.

A music, whose measure is timed from the music-stand of the moon, spreads flats of fireworks through the fields.

Movielanders enjoy drunkenness much more than love. Men know their women but they never see them so naked as when under the first full-moon.

The deities of the region, the black gods who laugh, on moonlit nights, with a hugely animal laugher, also enjoy the African Movieland night.

Stars fall down, stricken by the bullets of hunters whose shots cannot be heard; and nocturnal tigers and the tasseled tails of lions parade over the moon.

These cæsarean children of the moon commemorate their mother with a most frequent centenary. Their mother blesses them from the sky and breathes into them cinematographic inspiration for a long season.

This is their real and typical festival. Jacques mixes with the happy crowd and participates in the ceremony like everybody's brother-in-law; he looks through the moonlit night for the shelter of a grove.

In spite of the absolute liberty that night offers, couples still pursue each other clumsily. No one seems worn out by everyday passion. Ancient idyls come back to life.

Jacques, by Mary's side, is a lunar larva in the delirious festival.

The frogs go on rendering the night pleasant, making it real, with their snoring of nocturnal humidity: panting with life and dream, incongruous cry from one who is about to say something but decides, after all, to keep quiet.

Frogs interpret the agony of life.

"They entertain us with a nocturnal concert," says Mary from her corner. Jacques shelters her so well it seems that he has hidden her in his pocket.

Something is missing, something which would enliven the festival strewn under the immense moon of all the cinemas in the world. The garlands of Venetian lanterns and the music from the orchestra are not enough to give the unity of a frieze to all that is happening.

Suddenly there appears a luminous creature who, walking superbly through the darkness consecrated to the movies, forces all those who are lying supine in the black pots of night to sit up. She is the fairy or goddess of the cinema.

A long row of spectators gather on the path of the luminous woman; she transforms the half-slumbering festival into a chorus of song.

Everybody recognizes her: she is Virginia Cooper, the great pale figurant of the movies, she who, when facing Elsa, is like the remorse of a Movieland that had not made a star of her.

She is impregnated with the powerful lights of the studios;

that is why she has that cinema radiance, that bas-relief quality of film celluloid; she impresses them with her mere presence, by just putting on, in the shadow, her chemise of light.

CHAPTER XVIII

The Spoiled Child

MOVIELAND'S SPRING is aphrodisiacal.

Hearts become like steins full of beer.

Voluptuousness is shut in people's houses, and night is roasted on their grills. Vapors of pleasure escape from all windows.

Everybody spied on a strange couple composed of a famous child and the anxious brunette, Custodia. The Spanish Custodia had no family name, she was just Custodia, the perturbing Custodia, with circles under her eyes becoming blacker and blacker by dint of constant love-making.

Tommy, the prodigious child with the little suit and the lace collar, had been captivated by this woman with the kleptomaniac eyes. He wanted no toy but this woman with a nurse-like sweetness, who instead of being a wet-nurse was the nurse who had never been wet.

In a city like Movieland where nothing was scandalous, nevertheless this couple—a woman whose eyes bespoke preoccupation with a solitary pleasure and a child of rare intelligence—created a scandal.

Director Emerson once tried to persuade Tommy to stop this affair, but the little boy became so enraged and threatened so boisterously to quit his job, that the Director had to let it go.

This Spanish woman, made of cream and soot, rode with unbelievable effrontery in the car of the innocent child.

He lay on her breast while she manipulated that piece of an

armillary sphere called the wheel.

Sumptuous neckings, those between the child who earned a few thousand dollars a month and the Spanish woman, so clumsy on the screen but so perfectly built to be a rich boy's filly!

The child so beloved of the great public was as sensible as a man. That's why he understood everything and why he liked hard work so well. During performances he was so self-conscious that he was like a spoiled dandy of cathedral spaces.

Had he not known the secret of woman how could he give to his face the right and essential modicum of human hypocrisy?

His brow contained, under his roguish cap, a professional finesse whenever he played the rôle of the criminal child who while enjoying the pleasure of docile flesh makes of his women whores and slaves.

Tommy was not impudent but he was possessed with the desire of exploring warm marble.

He was like a prodigious child who instead of living on the complaisant petticoats of his first maid, prefers to play with her breasts.

Some of Tommy's sayings were quoted all over Movieland:

Tommy said today that "the elephant is a processional animal."

Tommy said today that "Movieland is the New Jerusalem and that in a few years not a single one of its bricks will remain."

Tommy said today that "footballs are the worst patched shoes in the world."

Tommy said today that "all cinema stars are *nouveau riche* miners."

Tommy said today that "pineapples are edible architectural ornaments."

Tommy said today that "accordions sound of sad cellars."

Tommy said today that "dogs are so filthy that they sissify men."

Tommy said today that "the enormous mouth of a hippopotamus is a letter-box for the mail addressed to Mesopotamia."

This child obsessed with definitions was in actual life a turbulent youngster.

Seated at his table, he was a restless, happy but domineering fetich. He was the offspring of no Movielander.

Where did he come from?

No one knew. No one demanded him back. His first flight was his flight to Movieland. He came directly there from a distant womb.

His contract with Director Emerson was quite amusing. He entered the Director's office, climbed on a table and began to chat with him with perfect familiarity, cutting papers all the time with the Director's shears.

That same afternoon the contract was signed. Tommy filled his first film with tenderness as if he were the representative of a world which makes one tremble for fear that cinema bandits will handle its only representative roughly.

In his luxurious, well-illuminated villa, where no visitors were ever allowed as if the child were suspicious of every one, Tommy resembled a child playing by the shore of a dangerous pond in which he might drown any moment.

Nevertheless freedom was so complete in Movieland that every one sympathized with the audacious youngster who did not waste time playing the silly, sterile games that other children like.

Through him everybody lived once again an ineffable childhood, imagining themselves to be children lying upon the morbid and sweet skin of a woman with no sanctities. . . .

CHAPTER XIX

Asylum for the Blind

Under the powerful lights of Movieland's big studio, eyes lose their intensity little by little and the glances of actors seem to come from the depths of remote galleries in the cloisters of sad convents.

All movie actors are in constant danger of losing their sight. Nothing can be done to prevent it and it is quite impossible for them to work wearing smoked glasses.

The sunlight from twenty thousand lamps burns the eyes out. The lachrymal bags suffer painfully, silver bromide pricks on their most sensitive veins.

But the eyes have to offer themselves to light, even when wounded; and in a season of great successes one of the most moving spectacles is when, in a holocaust to her public, the star burns her beautiful eyes in a blaze of light.

Poor women with their burnt-out retinas!

Some of them take care of themselves by remaining in the dark for a long period of time with their beautiful eyes hidden under cabbage leaves and ice compresses.

At times they want to work, blind as they are, but the intelligence of glances is of such paramount importance in the movies that they completely fail—they resemble owls.

In the movies, modulation of voice, diapason, musical and elegant diction, are all to be found in a pair of eyes. One can say that blind people are "cinematographically dumb." And they are sent to the Asylum for the Blind.

Their nurses try to console them by telling them that in the talkies blind actors will become the voices of films while actors with a pair of healthy eyes will be only the movable shadows.

The Asylum for the Blind resembles the Museum of Expression, but it is a less hellish madhouse, lodging discreet, peaceful, silent patients who have only been enslaved by the prisms of ecstatic madness.

The great blind stars of the cinema await, as the virtuous await delivery from Purgatory, the recovery of their sight. In the hope of renewing their vision, they keep their eyes in avid expectation of a miracle.

Many of these women were suddenly stricken blind when their tears, falling between their eyes and the powerful reflectors, became a sort of magnifying glass that burned their crystalline lenses.

The dark film of their blindness was constantly projected in clear and clean rooms, equipped with all the comforts that civilization can offer the blind: typewriters for the blind, kodaks for the blind, mirrors for the blind, etc.

Their eyes were still set in intense films bristling with the suggestive gems of their glances. It is only right that Movieland should do all that is possible for its blind.

Just now, the blind are all excited. They are going to take a walk through the moonlit fields—all of them, those who are totally blind and those who can still see a little, those who have become ankylosed in their blindness and those who struggle against it.

They are feverish. They begin to see; their eyes recognize the luminous and fantastic moon under which great films are shot.

Superproducer Sutton is going to use the blind for his superfilm, "The Revolt of the Blind."

The blind will have to run abysmal dangers, to meet each other, knife in hand, in a civil and fratricidal war. But the blind will not be able to see weapons which will, therefore, shine more glitteringly in front of solitary eyes. The public will be thrilled with this and no doubt the film will be placed in later years among the great masterpieces of the Museums of the Cinema.

Although, in this sad asylum—Movieland's only somber and tomorrowed spot—men and women are allowed to receive their lovers, it is pervaded by an old restlessness. Every one endeavors to find once more his best expression which, now impregnated with more recent expressions, will contain an accursed strangeness full of parenthetical scars. . . .

The day we visited the Asylum for the Blind, we noticed the habitually placid expression of those who cannot see, broken, now and then, by an attempt to strike a tragic attitude; the illuminated faces seem to be concentrated in their pupils.

CHAPTER XX

The Negroes

MOVIELANDERS KICK the negroes on their foreheads and crush them as if they were repugnant, white-eyed bullfrogs.

The boldest negroes who immigrate to Movieland from the neighboring forests believe that they can frighten white people with the terrible grimaces they extract from their white, diabolic Death's head teeth.

The head-crackers among Movieland's cops administer slaughter-house blows on the thick skulls of these rebels and kill them.

But some negroes succeed, remaining in Movieland as actors or as servants to white women.

Negro actors do wonders in tragic films, on whose thresholds they stand up like crocodiles erect on their tails. The negro expression resembles that of Cain when, standing on Abel's corpse, he made sure that Abel was good and dead.

Negro servants strive to prevent white folks from performing menial tasks in a city where civilization triumphs.

Prosperous negroes become shirt-makers—they go mad about bright polka-dotted shirts. They are also crazy about straw-hats which they suck blissfully, relishing the taste of sun and stormy-day that resides in humid straw.

Their ideas are short, limited—tiny lice from their kinky, woolly and impenetrable hair.

They bring an element of contrast into Movieland; they are the shadows of white people; they are zoological specimens that archangelicize white people.

They seem to have meditated a great deal and their wrinkled foreheads bear eloquent testimony to a meditative and intensely profound introspective life. But that's all bunk. All this reflective somberness is, merely, the harassing depression that their own blackness inflicts on them.

Their clock eyes gaze as if from behind a mask and such glances make of Movieland a cosmopolitan carnival.

Animals of life's morasses, obscure creatures, alert but incomprehensible, they can affect others only through the strength of their teeth, by biting their opponents to death.

The easy-going Movielanders find themselves somewhat restrained in the presence of negroes as if they had stepped into the cage of a domesticated wild beast. On what orgiastic night will the negroes' *coup de . . . patte* take place? When will they show their claws? On the least expected of nights, perhaps. The sweat from their blackness is a criminal sweat.

Under the big studio's electric lights they feel as if they were under a moonlit sky and their emotion increases as the light becomes more intense. They awake and stand up as if magnetized.

When the negroes act all the white film-people swoon away, thinking they are witnessing that religious moment when the moon urges the apocalyptic beast out of its sleep.

The grotesque, strangling hands of negroes make supplicant gestures as if the black God of their fears had appeared.

They look tragic even when playing in comic pictures, their deep wrinkles snarl like the meditation of caverns during the great night of the universe.

The robust negro, Simpson, is the sober and imposing boxing-star of the movies. He is hopelessly in love with Elsa. Everybody knows about it, even Max York. Max smiles at Simpson's melancholy, a negroid T.B. that seems to be consuming the dark inconsolable wooer.

A director took advantage of Simpson's negro passion while shooting a film of love and jealousy, and Simpson fluttered about Elsa like a black butterfly around a living flame.

Never had eyes and hands caressed so timorously, so furtively, barely skimming over Elsa's down. . . . The faded palms of his hands outlined simian caresses on the air, sketched upon space Elsa's complete structure.

Max, unnerved, like the husband of a female lion tamer when she enters the cage, caressed his revolver.

Simpson deserved to be crowned Emperor of all the Movieland negroes, for, during the performance, his turgescent gestures, his outlined caresses, resembled blessings.

Simpson became Max and Elsa's shadow. People attributed Max's faithfulness to this fact. Elsa threatened Max with this negro who crawled after her like a wounded man.

Elsa claimed that negroes dance very well, like undulations of black water. One day Simpson revealed to her the secret of their ambiguous, syncopated and staccato dance:

"Do you want me to try it for you?"

Elsa kept silent at his infectious request and from then on she ceased to praise negro dances.

Simpson was not a platonic lover who gets bored. He was the lover of the most perverse white women, those with a distinctive rubber-like flesh.

Simpson kept in his European house a fair-complexioned Algerian who became quite fond of him and who tried to dispel his home-sickness by playing the banjo for him.

The savage sounds of a banjo are echoes which emanate from the isolation of savage tribes.

The Algerian woman plays half-naked, her legs crossed, a position which makes her look fatter, especially her legs; for this posture augments what may be called the little arses on legs, those little bellies or "morbid posteriors."

A banjo has a dry melancholy which ought to be inadmissible as long as guitars exist. The banjo closes horizons and darkens gatherings.

The Algerian woman's broken songs recalled those tunes hummed by negroes somewhere in a remote plaza surrounded by huts. . . . The songs charmed the sleepy serpents in Simpson's patent-leather soul.

CHAPTER XXI

Mary's Death

Jacques Struk resembled the young man who goes away to study at a foreign university and receives a monthly check from his folks to cover his expenses.

Movieland was to him an exceptional adventure; he saw clearer than any one what took place there and he enjoyed thoroughly his dream-that-has-come-true, by living in the spirited city where the best cigarettes are smoked.

He was the student of no one knew what course and, accidentally, he had become the fiancé of one of Movieland's most radiant stars.

The ingenious and libertine Mary, who claimed that bidets are holy-water basins visited by women who want to purify themselves from the peccadillos of the day before, generously gave Jacques as a gift all the smiles that were left her after having decalcomaniaized thousands of them in the films—skyscrapers in which the actress becomes the neighbor of all windows.

She could not give him all that she would have wished, and her disillusioned talk showed how much she was unable to give him.

She suffered from an exhausted heart.

"I have used up all my soap. There hardly remains in me that wafer which remains in the soap-case after a cake of soap has stayed in water for a long while," she used to say despondently.

She was *really* very tired.

She came out nicely in the movies but her face was worn out

through cinematographic incontinence and a diabetes of expression brought confusion into her best gestures.

She complained of her prodigality. She regretted having appeared in a pornographic film which had been nicely monopolized by moneyed-men—a film in which she acted most obscenely, playing at love with a ferocious dog whose repulsive eyes seemed to contain a paradise of abjection.

"As long as that picture continues to be projected you will suffer the tortures of innumerable hells and despite all absolution your soul will remain impure," her conscience used to repeat to her.

Jacques wanted to cure her neurasthenia but Mary complained of his naïveté as of a troublesome thorn.

How difficult it is to redeem a person harassed by the remote influences surrounding a cinema star! Jacques suffered from unsociability, from a fluctuating moodiness capriciously controlled, as it were, by a uterus not different from that of a radio's loud speaker.

How was this felicitous, tremulous idyl going to end?

Marriage was not possible, nor remembrance. Distant gusts drove away Mary's memories, and whenever she returned home she succumbed to the little pushes that throw one gently upon the divans of absolute libertinism.

But one evening an unforeseen accident happened. Mary was playing in a film. She wore a hoop-skirt and she had bedecked herself with lace like the most ostentatious of princesses in the days of crinoline. She resembled one of those rare birds of rich plumage whose wings are so heavy that they cannot fly.

The film trembled with the emotion brought into it by this woman who promenaded all the bauble and gewgaw ornaments that a well-equipped dressing-table can offer.

To show off the strange lineaments of her countenance more advantageously she carried a lamp in her hand—a lamp which derived its light from an acetylene tank hidden under her hoop-skirt.

With every gesture, with every bow the hoop-skirt emitted sounds of coquetry, evoked bath-house nakedness, echoes of things moving within a dark bell. With their fresh tinkles they wanted to bring back to existence an irresurrectible life.

One may reconstruct ancient things on a modern lawn but one readily detects their falsity. Lawns are dated. A struggle takes place between the long hood from which the veils of medieval heroines hang, and the grass and the modern lights that belie their authenticity. There are subtle differences between the lights of contemporary beings and ancient life; recent lights anachronize the plot.

After the show Mary jumped into her car just as if she were coming from a masquerade ball. She lighted a cigarette and, while smoking it, she compromised the historical decency of hoop-skirts. It all reminded one of those Venetian carnivals where contemporary perversity should not be construed, on account of the disguises, as ancient perversity.

Her auto rebelled against this hoop-skirt which required a different setting, a tall back seat inlaid with mother-of-pearl.

She was comfortably seated, smiling a nostalgic smile as a woman of a remote age would have smiled to the men of today.

Suddenly she felt her blood boiling on her legs and she saw herself enveloped in flames. She was burning!

She knocked desperately on the glass and the chauffeur stopped immediately.

The stubborn door caught in opening and the lace of her hoop-skirt became excellent fodder for the flames.

She fainted. The chauffeur threw her on the ground and wrapped her in covers, cushions and even his own coat.

At last the flames were extinguished. But what harm has the fire done?

The chauffeur put her back in the car and rushed to the clinic. She was dead.

Director Emerson wired the chauffeur to take Mary directly to the cemetery, eight miles away, so as not to bring sadness to Movieland, the gay city.

CHAPTER XXII

Women. Divorces. Bathers. A Fox-Terrier.
A Shower of Parrots. The Crocodile.

MOVIELAND IS A CITY bubbling with grace where women try to surpass each other in freedom, in their gestures, their carriage, their beauty, their smiles, producing thus a most atrocious feline confusion.

The clear cut definition of types, gestures and eyes admits no synthesis.

Breasts are encased in satin. A great actress never considers them important. She puts them to rest. She ignores them and so makes them irresistible.

"I have breasts, but it's all the same to me," she seems to say, and then with contemptuous pride she adds: "That's for bathers to worry about."

They carry their very sweet breasts in their eternally spring-like gowns as if in soft little bags, like scapularies preserved in essences and perfumes.

Some are most insignificant but also most expressive, and women who have them smile on that account at those who have round breasts and whose thighs burst open their step-ins.

When the ingenues return from the studio they seem to be coming back from the conservatory; they take a rest, innocently, as if they were not suggestive, the temptresses of men without sweethearts.

Women have gone to a sylvan state and they have become

stronger and cleaner than most people, but more animal.

They differ among themselves only in their impromptus and their opinions are like little trivial lights.

It is from shop-windows they gather most of their stuff for conversation.

One of them standing by the cheesemonger's stall says:

"This shop looks like a wholesale rat store."

Another at a glove shop says:

"Gloves are an absolution. . . . They exist so that one may change sins. I feel like a virgin when I put on new gloves."

Another at a jeweler's:

"Diamonds ought to melt. . . . Their impassibility irritates me. I should like to chew them or cast them in my champagne to see if they can thaw."

Fictitious glycerine tears are ill-becoming to their serene eyes. They are like the last raindrops from one of those storms that leave in their wake a too-beautiful day.

Glycerine was useless in the following case:

There was a woman who could not cry and when she tried could only grimace. The film was retaken six times in the attempt to get tears or, at least, some passably authentic congestion from her. But all in vain.

At last they resorted to the absurd onion. Onion juice was sprinkled all over her face and, thanks to that, a few tears came and, with them, perfection to that dry and charming beauty.

These onion tears are a powerful argument against the cinema. They bring out its falsity and secretly vilify it, expressing all the ferocious hypocrisy of its wily griefs.

The greatest plastic beauty in the world lives in Movieland.

The Plastic Beauty moves about a house full of black curtains and the milky light from condensed-milk electric bulbs.

She lives, naked, in her velvety house.

As one of her more spiritual lovers used to say:

How can she conceal the terrible microbes that graze on her? It seemed, really, that microbes, respecting her beauty, had become repressed, intimidated, like tame tigers, though they would have been doubly cruel to any one else.

"Doctor, have I all the diseases possible?"

"All."

"Good! I can now give myself up to any one tranquilly. Nobody can pass anything on to me."

"You need only fear negroes."

"Why?"

"They have maladies that only devotion to their black idols can cure . . . maladies born in mud and in the most appalling misery."

She has a hesitantly haughty smile as one who has done some harm and is afraid of doing it again.

She has a mouth so poisonous that it does not dare to shut itself; its dry lips cannot close over the teeth—a mouth falsely timid and arid that remains open through sheer vacuity.

Just as all men are willing to fight a round or two, or fence a while, all women are ready to fall in love with some one.

The redoubtable women are those who have been whipped with a wet towel for health's sake, to get back that schoolgirl complexion.

They never try to make real or touching the remoteness in their eyes. They inject into them a becoming romanticism but one that is never in harmony with the rest of their faces.

They play the rôle of raped girls so as to be noticed.

Some of them are not aware of their beauty, but others are so much so that, when endowed with the greatest cinematic charm in women: shoulders, they smile with them. . . . They give their shoulders all the attractions that excite desire; they hide themselves behind a fan so as to reveal only their malicious shoulders.

Every one of them has been shipwrecked and has died a number of times. They have seen themselves stiff, pale with death, their corpses abandoned on the stage. In the movies the dead do not get up after the public applause. They have, on that account, the cynicism of survivors after oblivion.

Authentic Venetian women exhibit the animality of an uncertain art in Movieland's streets.

In Movieland beauty produces a certain sadness, like that produced in noble spirits when they attend a game of tennis. Everything happens simply, with a simplicity which white stockings bring out; breasts are the rubber balls in the game of love.

So as to intensify their expressions they take cocaine. They thus put more soul into the films, but cocaine dominates and destroys them.

But what of it?—when they bequeath to distant audiences their immense eyes as a remembrance. Spectators are attracted by these eyes that look toward an abyss.

Many cinema widows are more dead than alive. Death arises to take advantage of their mourning, to watch their attitudes, to observe their pale, blond beauty amid black graves.

The horizon becomes full of the dead who raise up their heads. In the widows' private rooms the walls are papered with eyes.

Some actresses are aware of the impurity of white dresses, of the frenetic, contagious impurity of white skirts.

Whiteness carries them from one place to another with alcoholic avidity, making them cross bridges leading nowhere, laughingly, with a laughter that harmonizes with their white dresses and with the affectation of their pale hypocrisy.

Intrepid navigators of the street, they leave behind them the anxious wake of their whiteness.

Everything was frank in Movieland and there was not the hypocrisy of those open air dances in which gawky, tender-thighed young ladies conceal, for some pragmatic reason, what they might give as the ewes give to the male lambs of the flock, and then later on play about as much as they please. To frolic in the confines of an ideal Movieland, without losing the cobwebs of purity . . . such is the provocation of unchaste virgins!

The day after a marriage the public expects the news of the divorce of the newly married as a sort of expiation and compensation.

The moving picture sections of newspapers print with gusto a thing like this: "Alma Rod and Thomas Abrel have asked for a divorce."

These divorces make the entire world happy: one learns that the star is free again, and that, therefore, new movements and new possibilities may be anticipated in the common skies.

Immediately after the marriage spies hurry to find out when the quarrel leading to divorce will come.

There are spies behind all the curtains; maids are false maids employed by divorce trusts which always keep track of that moment when boredom begins.

There are so many divorces in Movieland that when, for instance, Colon Bretanza and Julienne Barry got married, the two divorcés each presented a long catalogue of former husbands and wives.

Colon Bretanza, former husband of:	Marion Bulwer
	Carmen Dorado
	Mary Bogan
	Constance Farman
	Lillian Naldi
Julienne Barry, former wife of:	Jack Mar
	William Sux
	Carlos Moral
	King Walter
	Herbert Crane

"Will they be able to include the names of all their husbands and wives in their death-notices?" asked a wise guy.

Movieland has an extraordinary repertory of eyes. One is compelled to read the papers in the streets not to get drunk with so many cognac, curaçao, peppermint, and gin eyes.

How many pure, aristocratic, champagne-colored eyes there are!

The pigeonholing mind is interrupted when facing indefinable eyes. There are changeable green eyes which seem to be looking at a landscape from the window of an express train.

There are eyes that shine like a crystal blossom upon which the shadow of the lashes falls like a water-shadow on a mirror. There are eyes of a lost patience, eyes like a roadster disappearing in the distance, eyes like a bridge with clinging vines, eyes . . .

The dog-days have arrived. The female inhabitants of Movieland wear their bathing costumes all day long and look forward to taking a dip in the water.

Washed and cleansed of the soot of virginity, they scatter about them, instead of the aroma of their puzzling sex, a sweet, ideal and peaceful atmosphere, reminiscent in its saintliness of a walk in an orchard full of delectable fruits.

Those men who read in the shadow of their gardens instead of being mortified by sexual preoccupations can go on reading without losing their page and enjoy every single word in the book. Movieland is at this season the only place in the world where a book can be read.

Constant bathers with field-glasses around their necks, so as to see what is happening in the distance, scatter that maritime odor which, in women, is stronger than the sea's; but others, uncowled, rid themselves of the monstrosity of bathing costumes.

Some of them with their striped suits recall happy games with striped balls.

An ideal series of feminine-colored hoops spreads in the air concentrically.

These morbid and childishly playful bathers are used as illustrations even by orthodox magazines. They hypocritically reproduce these Eves with the dangerous curves, polished and aggravated by the brilliant water, as if they were presenting something quite admissible which could stand the close inspection of any decent family. But it is only to poke fun at human hypocrisy and its subterfuges that they bring to the attention of the serious public these peccant silhouettes.

These magazines are kept open the longest at the pages on which they appear!

Among the sirens that undress on Movieland's beaches there are real sirens, as deceitful as those who, according to Homer, tried to vamp Ulysses with their songs, or whom, according to Pliny, Roman patricians claim to have seen at Cadiz, or those whom numerous witnesses declared to Emperor Maurice they saw by the delta of the Nile, or like that siren whom Dutch women taught to make the sign of the cross.

Those who are most tarred by the sea-water are the most plastic. They seem to be made of marble or basalt polished by the centuries. It is their bare legs that jeopardize these creatures' marmoreal or basaltlike quality, for bare legs reveal pores that are indisputably fleshy, unevennesses for which the uneven fingers of their moulder is responsible. Their legs disclose that the images are made of flesh and bone.

When too many bathers appear in a photograph the feminine image loses its value, and it seems as if the crowd on the beach is a school of seals or dolphins. When men come on the scene, it becomes neutralized. For when *they* appear in the picture, one realizes immediately these men are *the* lucky ones and one gets envious and stops looking.

At times, among the girls there is one that can dance, one who, separating from the crowd, stands up and begins to dance a *pas seul,* the dance of the dolphin on the sea.

With her suit clinging to her body, she improvises the dance of Venus awakening, or that of the wave transformed into the Immaculate Conception.

It is extremely difficult to weave a dance in the midst of open nature by the sea, for the dancer must try very hard to focus the eyes of the spectators.

Typists with no typewriters, the chorus girls of the movies are happy and independent. They have no preoccupation but seeing the days flow by.

Typists of the minutes, they tickle each one of them, and let it go at that. After that, they feel nourished, loved and outlined by curves as happily insolent as their hips.

But beside these happy typists with no typewriters and with no office hours, there are beautiful and exhausted women who, instead of being aged or mature, are tired, very tired. . . .

A fox terrier smokes his pipe like a sailor with drooping lips, reminding one of a face in which a single tooth shines.

He is insured for $20,000 and carries as many medals on his collar as do superstitious women.

Everybody counts on him and women even cast facetious glances at him as if meaning to say caressingly, "You big bum!"

On this African corner of Movieland there is a touch of Eden.

Its particular curiosity is that, besides its good climate, it becomes at times a forest of parrots, filled with a fluttering of bright colors.

It seems as if a fantastic decorator has adorned the city. At a first glance one would think the city was wearing a varicolored blouse. Soon after, the parrots fly off to their forest and the city remains sad, naked, bald of colors.

But Movieland's most fantastic animal, one who differs from all imaginable animals, is a crocodile that once upon a time had to be a dinosaur; that is to say, during the making of Movieland's most impressive prehistoric film he had to wear a bony crest and imitate a dinosaur by walking majestically and adapting his gestures to the orders of the stage director.

CHAPTER XXIII

Parties at Elsa's House

Elsa's house was brilliant every night. Her crystal chandeliers were frozen raindrops dancing in the air.

The balconies of the great drawing-room opened on a half-lit terrace. There were delightful parties, at which Elsa's Russian wolfhounds slept like princes on the divans, while the French poodles slumbered in the arm-chairs. They were school boys in lace collars, students in a great college for aristocratic dogs.

Moonlight nights on Elsa's terrace were never to be forgotten.

The moon of Movieland was a huge balloon anchored to earth by a thousand endless strips of film. It was a pier glass set high in the sky for women who were as transparent at night as though they had put on a diaphanous gown in the first bright sun of spring. Many of them, despairing of being able to see themselves in so high a mirror, took out vanity cases.

That Easter moon seemed about to lay Easter eggs filled with favors of platinum and diamonds for the delight of the ladies of the evening.

When the dew began to fall they went into the drawing-room. The floor was so highly polished that one almost feared to drown in it.

"I don't know why," said the absurd Klin, "but I seem to feel cellos throbbing in the depths of that floor."

"It has the same effect on me. These rooms are always stately and alone, or just about to welcome their mistress who enters trailing a long white robe."

"The furniture is reflected in the parquet like black poplars in the waters of a canal."

"Here, Doré, you say something about the floor."

"The clock gleams in it like the moon in a pool."

"Too much of the poplars in that," Elsa objected.

"Then I'll say it is as gorgeous as a mahogany staircase opening into a theater foyer."

"Bravo. That's better."

Max York, who felt called upon to instruct them, expounded the daily press. All the newspapers were full of a raid made by a dozen burglars who had held up a dance and robbed every guest. "I would like to have been there, even though it cost me my wallet."

"Imagine doing it so well without having rehearsed it!"

"Imagine seeing faces filled with real terror and real surprise, in place of the imitation emotions we register."

"Imagine knowing how to avoid taking any jewels that might stick as they came off, and picking off necklaces with the careless grace of a peddler showing rosaries."

"They've caught the burglars," Max said.

"What a shame," said Elsa. "I'd like to know how movies come out in real life."

"Better than in our studios, my dear. Among the jewels stolen at the Heuton reception was a most curious emerald. It seemed to hold a garden in its heart, and although that made it less valuable as a precious stone, it gave it added charm as a curiosity. 'Even though they take all the stones out of settings and sell them separately,' Dorothy Heuton told the police, 'that emerald will betray them. There is no other like it in the world. Fantastic in itself, the arrangement of the garden is absolutely unique. The burglars will think they can sell it as they would any other stone, and the attempt will ruin them.' As a matter of fact that is exactly what happened. The police waited for the Garden emerald to appear on the market. Finally one of the burglars brought this heaven-marked stone to a small jewelry shop. The police arrested him, caught his three accomplices, and now have hopes of recovering all the stolen jewels."

"What a deep breath the strangled women will take!"

"Strangled?"

"Yes. A woman whose necklace is stolen is as breathless until she gets it back as though she had been strangled."

Every one wondered about the robbery for a while, then they talked of the movies. They never went to see them. They would have had to be desperate to the point of madness to enter the door of a movie theater, but they talked of them incessantly. They even used the cinema as a bogey with which to frighten naughty children, as though it were the worst monster in Movieland. The only people there who look at pictures are certain sad men called testers who examine the condition of every film before it is sent out to the world.

Tonight Max York was furious because they were commonly spoken of as screen figures.

"Screen figures! Screen figures!" he protested. "I am tired of hearing that. It makes us sound like those cut-outs which are silhouetted on the edge of the screen—Chinese shadows on a Chinese film. I feel as though I were doomed to be a shadow without a soul in a movie made at home."

"It's the truth. I've always thought the same thing," said Elsa. "What dreadful person first called it a screen, which blocks things off, when it should have been named a window flung open to the future?"

"But it seems to me," some one disagreed, "that something which is really a screen can't be called a curtain or a sheet."

"We are spinning a hank of celluloid yarn which winds itself around the entire globe," Cak Foy broke in. "Every one spins something—life is just that absurd. According to a statistician who calculated it in the bobbin of his head, the strip of film which was produced last year would go around the earth four times."

"The thing we are loosing on the world," said the most disillusioned of the group, "is a gigantic tapeworm."

"How sad our dream world is!" said Albert Bojer.

"No. You cannot call it a world of dreams," Dr. Haidin sprang to its defense. He was famous as a champion of the movies. "That is a bad comparison. Things go very badly in a world of dreams. You try to strike a light and it doesn't work. There are all sorts of blunders, and if you examine dreams closely you will see that they are very seldom finished."

"Things may go badly in dreams, but there are always the movies!"

"The works of the great masters of literature live gorgeously in the films that have been made of them," said one of the cast.

"Don't you believe it. When they come to life they are lost. There is no fragrance left in a book after a film has been made of it. Poor authors! They are seduced by a siren who first muddles things up, and then dries the life out of them."

"Then you don't think that a great novel is improved by being filmed?"

"Not in the least. It is destroyed, rendered null and void, sent back into the darkness of the unimagined."

The thing that pleased Elsa's guests most was the fact that they felt themselves so far away from those worshiping multitudes who would have liked to attend the making of movies just as they attend the playing of a ball game, in hordes great enough to inundate the place. One would think the mere size of those crowds would make them ashamed of themselves.

Difficult problems were set forth on the blackboard of the sky.

"What relation is there between the cinema and the safety razor?"

"I've often thought of that."

"There is undoubtedly something movie-like in shaving with a Gillette."

"Yes. Perhaps after many days of shaving the film will begin to click into shape—every blade a closeup."

Then they talked of women.

"Tell me something which will prove the retiring nature of woman," begged a gallant man with a rich, fruity note in his voice.

"Everything does. But if you want something conclusive, is anything more so than the fact that a woman can make love for a long time with her hat on? When she gives her last kiss to the man who has killed himself for her, she does it in a hat. The final love scene always shows her with her head completely hidden."

Conversations broke off as soon as they were commenced, and they all ended in gossip.

"The old boy makes an awful fuss over her. He'll make a star out of her before he's through."

"She is the kind you find asleep on park benches, head resting on the back, wriggling and scratching in her sleep as though she had stirred up endless ant hills."

As the night went on they all grew transcendental. It was probably sleepiness.

"You are not interested in the hereafter?" Edna Blake asked Elsa.

"No. Poised as we are, half way between shadow and reality, we know no hereafter."

"Then we should dedicate ourselves solely to living?"

Between three and four in the morning the party finally ended.

CHAPTER XXIV

The Perfect Drunkard, the Chameleon, and the Movie Mustache

One of the best paid people in all Movieland is a good drunkard.

All the drunks in the world clamor for a chance to act in the films of Movieland's two famous companies, Circle and Cosmogony.

A good moving picture drunkard is a very difficult thing to find. He is not a drunkard who reels and staggers about, throwing two pale locks back from a receding forehead. No. He is a drunkard in full command of himself, a presidential drunkard, capable of presiding over a world congress of drunkards.

The perfect drunkard has complete control over himself. He goes through melancholy and repulsive sprees and emerges utterly untouched. His type is ignoble, but it is a meditative ignobility, convinced of its own worth, and always hiding a caress in the thicket of its beard.

Your ideal toper never loses his equilibrium; on the contrary, the load he has taken on races into his veins thickening the red wine of his blood and renovating it: venous to arterial blood, exhausted wine to new.

Not much white wine in that blood. It is full of good red corpuscles. This ideal boozer enters seriously into the spirit of the cinema; his presence sets off the rest of those palefaced drinkers who only swallow water which has been absolved from its original sin; that is, boiled and aerated.

When the perfect drunkard lays a hand on his white victim the whole film trembles. The truth of the world stands forth in all its nakedness.

The common drunks employed by certain film companies make jerky pictures reeking with ancient farce and stale melodrama.

The perfect drunkard, melancholy and impassive, is as true an example of the selection of species as is a perfect gentleman, who would not for a moment descend to the criminal grossness of the alcoholic.

They found one perfect drunkard in Movieland. They called him "Pernot," which is the French trade name for absinthe, and his impudent son, who disobeyed him, insulted him and robbed him, they named "Pernot fils"

On his office mantel there was a black idol called Pernot's god. Its ugliness fascinated him. It made him wonder if in the dark forests there were gods corresponding to that of Europeans, gods who might be better adored than theirs, gods who would be worthy of his stupendous vices.

It was a cynical office. Apparently crowded with books, it contained nothing but rows of book-backs concealing a deadly depth of empty compartment.

"This way I had only to pay for the end bindings," Pernot used to say.

"And how a row of good titles does encourage meditation!"

That livid, spiteful, crafty face, which at times scared even its owner when he saw it in the mirror, was the thing that triumphed in the movies. The absinthe, which he drank in ever increasing amounts, twisted his head with a kind of alcoholic neuritis. He was swollen with unassimilated absinthe. His heart must have been like those preserved in flasks of alcohol in a laboratory. Poor hearts, even though they lived in the bodies of abstemious folk, they come to a drunkard's end.

Theodore Palmer was a different person every day. Utterly a creature of Movieland, he was a true human chameleon.

His creation of various types was amazing on the screen, and even more so in real life. After sitting beside him at a dinner table for hours some old friend of his would recognize him with an astonished:

"Why, Theodore, is that you?"

Palmer's whole psychology changed with every rôle. Each new character he assumed emphasized the distance he had gone from what was once his own personality.

He told interviewers: "I must know what rôle I am going to play a month or two before the filming of the first scene, so that I may devote myself to living that new type with all its consequences—its sordidness, its extravagances, or whatever it demands. The soul is as changeable as the face, and may be made gay or austere, ambitious or terrible."

His hats, his clothes, his mustache, his glasses, his manner of looking at things—all were different.

His peculiar talent made him an ideal actor. Never was he the same, always he was some one else. The thing he loathed above all else was the failure to contradict himself, the monotony of holding the same opinion today that he held the day before yesterday.

Chameleon that he was, he claimed to be surprised at his own reflection in the dim mirrors of show windows. Instead of nodding at himself, he never returned his own salutation as he went past the shadowed glass.

His pretense penetrated so deeply into his life that even outside the great hothouses of the movie studio he was always an actor, a man who sat on the terrace of his pet café as though he were another person, a tired stranger who unlaced his shoes to teach patience to his rebellious feet.

The chameleon man peopled the imagination of his neighbors with the most varied human types. Every one agreed that the types which lasted longest and were most impossible to forget were those extraordinary beings which far exceeded reality. And even after he had finished with them they still lived on, all jumbled together in a strange movie existence of their own.

The chameleon actor will live for a long time. He renews himself each season. He appears before the world as a type so different that no detail of it is ever twice alike. "The things which age us," he said once, "are the ideas which grow old in us, the convictions which are never given up, the memories which bore us."

So complete is the success of the chameleon, so perfect is he in his metamorphoses, that even his creditors do not recognize him, and it has even happened that one of them has made him a new loan.

What condition, what type, what art is necessary for success in Movieland?

Most of all a mustache. A tiny mustache, a nervous mustache, a most particular mustache, the mustache never before known among mustaches, a mustache so original that even if the whole world should imitate it, it would not matter. For the model has a latent life of its own. It is accompanied by an entire system of expressions, actions, sidewise glances, thoughts which shine luminous on the photographed face to which it belongs. It is sufficient in the movie world to have a mustache no bigger than that of a new-born baby boy. It is more valuable than all the booming oratory and all the dramatic tricks with which the actor's art ties itself up in knots.

CHAPTER XXV

Experimental Movies

THERE ARE IN MOVIELAND certain experimenters who enjoy a separate studio, the so-called "Studio Intime."

The actors who have a thirst for creating congregate in that simple glass house and there invent such surprising films as the one in which the only characters are two eyes which move in curdled darkness.

This studio is a kind of miniature conservatory in which only the rarest species are cultivated. Among its experiments is the poetic film.

The entire picture is governed by a poem which is neither transcribed nor projected on the screen, but which gives that inimitable rhythm of a cinema creation.

"What is the particular charm of this picture?" they ask the carefully selected first night audiences. It lies in the fact that the very expressions assumed by the actors are taken over by the audience. Astonishing, these experimental movies!

In true movie fashion, their titles always involve the unusual and the unexpected. "The Unmet Hour," "Eyes of the Planets," "The Unknown Temple," "The Hand That Fails," "The Cabaret of the Dead," "The Battle of the Glow Worms," "The Soul's Amulet."

They also create things which are both more serious and more general.

Objects in such films have something of the quality of things called up from the spirit world by mediums.

Clocks, for example, play rôles of their own. In one film

there was a never-to-be-forgotten clock that stood over the fireplace. On its luminous face there appeared these words, which for some reason or other became harrowing in the course of the play: "Learn to lean on this clock, which marks our life, so that afterward you may learn to have all the sorrow I merit."

A certain incongruousness, pulled together by invisible bands, dominates these experimental films. The most widely diverse things take on a common fervor.

It becomes apparent that the movies have many secret resources.

In that crystal chamber devoted to exploring the future they have arrived at a cinematography of souls, a cinematography in which a ribbon of sensitized celluloid records the life of ectoplasmic beings. Called up out of the spirit world by ouija boards, these disembodied ones are thrust onto the stage while camera men record their wonder and their unforgettable reunions.

How many Francesca Bertinis of the other world mimed the sorrows of spirit harps! Those delicate nostrils swollen with weeping!

The writers of experimental films are set apart from those who succeed in the present cinema. They are not so much writers as confectioners of a thing as yet undefined. In order to find the stubborn germ of thought they must seek strange inspirations. Some of them write their plots in garages, seeking fame in the odor of gasoline. They search for a reality as swift and dependable as that of a good automobile. Driven by the famous gas of human passions, searching for inspiration which shall be authentic and worthy of the middle class audiences to which they cater, they crouch under a car as though they were mechanics on a repair job, or children nourished by the grease of its udders.

The things which are hidden with the greatest care by the huge workshops of Movieland are those inventions which might upset the great stream of classic films in which Movieland capitalists have invested their fortunes.

There is nothing unusual about that. Discoveries which affect anything already exploited on a huge scale have always been hidden. For a long time the vaults of the great phonograph companies have held imprisoned a model of a self-winding phonograph. The very radio companies themselves were jailed because they were going contrary to official plans.

The experimental movies serve as a shield for a new invention which cost Movieland $600,000. It is well guarded, for some day it will abolish the present type of production as though an earthquake and a great tidal wave struck together at the foundations of Movieland.

The day that some catastrophe—a general strike, the failure of Cosmogany—forces Movieland to become something else than what it is, its directors will put that carefully guarded invention to work, and the whole movie spectacle will be turned upside down.

A little is known about the new miracle, but only very vaguely. Some discharged employee failed to guard the seal of silence that surrounds new inventions, and let fall a hint of the movie of the future and its possibilities.

Its basis is the overcoming of spectator immobility, and the possibility of moving him toward the field of truth without his having to live it with all the consequent dangers of the drama and its incidents. He will always be the spectator, but he will be moved forward toward events.

The spectators will be thrown into a seeing sleep, and carried straight to the mountainous heights of true landscape and true argument. By means of electric, radiographic, and fifth dimensional forces in the new apparatus, the audience will enter the play through a paleolithic funnel which takes the place of the old screen. Their sleeping bodies will stay in their seats, well guarded by the police.

There will be three intermissions to give imaginations a rest so that they may be eager for the next scene. The audience will rub their eyes like people waking from a long sleep, surprised to see each other again.

Then the new projector will restore the mass of things to the spirits drawn in by the cone, will pick up the audience, and transport it to the scene of its new adventures.

The memory of these films of the future will be much more vivid to people who have seen them than the memory of pictures projected on the old screen, or even than the memory of dreams.

CHAPTER XXVI

Pilgrimages, and He Who Came From Afar

ALTHOUGH MOVIELAND is in the midst of an inhospitable desert and is a very difficult place to find, its doors are besieged by a constant stream of pilgrims.

Automobiles of fans who come from far away pass many travelers bound for the great city. Among them are young girls who beg rides from men journeying along.

This was the way that Eleanor came to Movieland. Today she is one of those women who put more seduction into their eyes—seduction for millions of men—than they put drops of belladonna.

Among those who come to Movieland in continual hordes are certain young men who think themselves strong enough to lift a house with one hand. Admired by their friends or their fellow employees, they take the long road to the city of their dreams. When they arrive they are exhausted. The moment they come into its terrible light they realize their blunder, and the three days which Director Emerson allows for seeing the city they spend staring into shop windows, ashamed of their battered shoes.

Day by day new shiploads of North American tourists arrive in Movieland. Automobiles pasted over with windshield stickers reading "To Movieland" pick them up at the nearest port.

They all act as though they were strangers to each other. They are most curious and diverting folk. The old women are silent. The young women wear great glasses, and coats unsuited to the spring climate. One rheumatic old thing is half paralyzed, but she still has energy enough to go around the world. There are dirty-faced girls in rough wool coats who manage somehow to clothe neat legs in gray stockings.

The automobile caravan stops in the plaza of Movieland as though it were the end of a long road, and every one sheds the immobility of the past days. They shake their linen dusters as ducks shake their backs.

"We do not come to pry too much into your lives. It would be quite impossible for us to remain here, nor would we take you away. We come only to look about and to take a few snap shots," they seem to say.

They speak the same language, they have traveled for days on the same ship united by the constant danger of settling into the sea together, yet they pass each other silently, looking the other way, and go to congregate anew around automobiles gathered together in other cities of the world.

Among those pilgrims who came by the short cuts that end in Movieland, in a crowd of masculine flappers and engineers out of a job, there appeared a stranger possessed of romanticism and adoring a star.

Thus he reached the home of Virginia, that great actress who plays sweet women. He was a mere boy, his face illumined with that burning passion which kindles fire in the loftiest of ladies.

Virginia listened to him. She was a slender woman, vivid and alluring, possessed of those vigorous curves which are the essence of seduction. She made the timid youth sit down. He told her his unimportant name as if she, who clothed everything with interest, might give it some value.

Abel, come from a great distance, gazed hungrily at that delicate and athletic woman. Her arms—feminine and at the same time strong—gave her somewhat the air of a circus performer constantly engaged in the exercise of physical power. Her wrist watch was a toy set on an arm which might hug one to death.

The slightest hint of coyness in those arms sent men completely mad, for they should surrender without any reservation. They were slow-moving, almost phlegmatic; but ruffles or bracelets gave them a frantic, nervous quality.

Her gestures, long famous in the movies, had the beauty and the life of things which do not pass.

"Have you changed your eyes?" Abel asked Virginia.

"Changed my eyes?"

"Yes. The question sounds rude, but I couldn't help asking. Your real eyes—the eyes you exchanged for these—were large enough, but they were not these artificial, made-up movie eyes. There is undoubtedly a hinge in the back of them. Some doctor knows—"

"And did you come to tell me that?"

"No. I came because I was tired of waiting in empty movie houses, hearing the final curtain drop without having succeeded in seeing anything. One would doubt having eaten asparagus if it weren't for the pile of stems, which are the vegetable's cigarette stubs. So I was tired of being thrown out of movie theaters which held no trace of you, houses which fooled us as though we were idiots."

Sorry for the credulous youth, Virginia tried to undeceive him.

"Why did you come? There is the same emptiness here, even though our mornings seem as gay as those on lovely beaches. We are merely forlorn little bugs lost in a wilderness of lonely beds. I could not give you anything even though I wished to, and especially since you ask so much, since you hope so much of me."

"You cannot say that, you who are so beautiful, who have given your incomparable loveliness to the films."

"My poor friend, you are as ignorant as a child. Our delicacy, our smiles, are for advertising purposes only. We sell our souls to the bright lights. We can do nothing but play the picture as it is written for us, being always oblivious to everything else. I swear to you that the great lights blot out the very soul's beliefs."

Being neither rich, poor, nor a screen fan, the new lover gave Movieland a new concept of love. He accompanied Virginia everywhere, wrapped in his dreams, a new representative of far away romanticism.

CHAPTER XXVII

Movie Fat Men and Carlos Wilh

IN THE MOVIES, the fat man takes on an insolence even greater than that which he shows on the terraces of beer gardens when he opens his coat and flaunts his enormous paunch.

Fat men floated all about Movieland. It upheld their exaggerated roundness. They were like buoys for those passers-by who were too thin or who were fainting from weakness.

They were justified by the movie belief: "You must have fat men to amuse thin ones. There is nothing so pleasing to a thin man, nothing which so compensates him for that thinness of his which whispers of death, as seeing the bobbing, barrel-like silhouette of a fat man."

Movieland also believes that fat men, like custard pies, are the mascots that save bad films from failure.

Their shamelessness about their bulk is atrocious. Apparently it comes from having wallowed in drunken laziness.

Uncombed, making fat spoiled children out of themselves, they possess neither the decency which would impel them to be apologetic, nor the desire to go on a diet as does all the rest of humanity, who constantly try to lose weight.

These movie fat men are sweaty, slovenly folk, given to daring impertinences which make the whole crowd laugh.

The important thing to find out is whether a fat man is full of good or evil. Both kinds seem to be equally funny; the good man is completely good, while the other is excessively malign, his instincts and his passions all bound up together in a dreadful confusion.

There is one fat man who never thinks of other people, who eats them up and laughs while he is digesting the world, but on the other hand there is another silent and thoughtful fat man whom every one holds in high esteem.

Movie fat men are usually vulgar beasts who make a profession of their fatness.

When they stop in the street it is as though they were on wheels weighing a ton and shod with balloon tires.

At times there is something very sordid about them, even in the mussy and mirthful type.

Some of these fat men have their paunches full of asthma and bad intentions. All the rotten vegetation of an old irrigation tank lies bubbling in their bellies, sending its corruption up to the minds above.

These movie fat men have no discretion whatsoever. One may be obese and still be a silent passer-by, winning respect and sympathy. But if one is obese and slovenly, anxious to be a cotillion leader of dropsical dances, the result is abominable.

Abominable? Yes, but not to the great public. It laughs all the harder at the fat man grown vulgar, paunchy and unwieldy.

There are various fat men in Movieland given to putting on airs. The most prominent among them is Carlos Wilh, tall and huge, always carrying the dreamy expression of one who used to win prizes in fat baby contests.

Carlos Wilh had no consideration for anything or anybody. Everything was fish to his net. His only comments on things that happened about him were the dimplings and grimaces of a huge child.

He treated women with the spoiled air of an overgrown baby.

The fat Wilh deprived himself of nothing. His stein of beer always stood foaming in front of him. A captive balloon of Movieland, he went balancing his enormous bulk from picture to picture.

It was hard for his chubby face to simulate a smile. He had the absorbing insolence of a low point of view, and his eyes suffered from the interior glare of his instincts.

Women laughed at him; only the very vulgar fell under the sway of this joke, giving themselves up to the influence of the grotesque without fear or shame for the asthmatic insufficiency of the cultivator of fat.

Everything in Carlos Wilh's life combined to stuff him. Even his diet was fattening, for if he got thin he would lose all his contracts and be as flat as one of those balloons which circus clowns let loose and puncture as they play with the public.

In the gay movie morning Carlos Wilh arrayed himself in light garments, and adorned his button hole with a flower. His admirers would have loved tiny dogs just as much, and in the same way, as they loved him. They fanned him with tiny fans given them in hairdressing shops.

At every party he spun about in the midst of a whirl of jokes. Shipwrecked in the pool of his flesh, he sputtered like a skyrocket in the water.

The most refined, most puritanical women of Movieland delighted in taking a public vacation from too great delicacy, and went off with Carlos Wilh into a dithering nonsense spree.

He was an octopus who reached out long waving tentacles for all beauty, and he liked to have every one know it.

One might well say that Carlos Wilh, boasting of his deeds, dislodged the spiritual quality of Movieland and shoved it away with one violent thrust of his barbarous great weight.

The movie fat men have about them something of the grossness of wild boars. At one and the same time they are giants and blow fish, and then they are gentlemen who, seated on the terraces of their pet cafés, jog up and down on their knees all the little girls who come near them.

CHAPTER XXVIII

Fake Bull-Fighters. The Shadow of a Tail-Coat. The Visionary.

THE SWAGGERING CHARACTERS of Movieland are solid and tangible ghosts who have found in its unreality jobs ideally suited to their laziness. In all this blustering crowd the fake bull-fighters are supreme. Wind-bags that they are, they are the scorn of all true toreros who may at any moment move into that part of the bull ring which bears the shadow of sorrow, and be buried in its sudden tragedy.

Each day there are more of these cinema bull-fighters. They are both proud and gay—proud because they can wear gorgeous costumes heavy with gold, gay because even though they dress like generals they do not have to go to war and their clothes will never suffer the somber stains that disfigure even the underwear of real toreros.

The fake bull-fighters of the screen walk boldly through all the streets of Movieland.

"Who is that?" the tourists ask.

"That," answer the guides, "is a bull-fighter."

The imitation bull-fighters, about as Spanish in type as a Canadian, live the lives of true toreros. Their boots are shined ten times a day, they drink three vermouths, they pinch the pits out of their olives after quartering them.

For them the day is always bright, without danger and difficulty, and free of the necessity of traveling. The life of a bull-fighter who never needs face the shocks of danger is a marvelous thing.

Movie bull-fighters need no assistance, and not being called on to kill, they need no sword boys. Their whole reputation as toreros lies in their brilliant trappings and in their eyebrows, which are heavy and black above eyes the color of asphalt. Their gorgeous costumes are always ready for immediate wear, hanging at home over the backs of chairs as though they were the clothes of firemen awaiting a call.

The movie bull-fighters will never suffer that terrible pain of a first goring, unless they meet with an injury in an automobile accident.

At times the movie bull-fighters put on gala dress just to go out on the street, and wrap themselves in their brilliant cloaks as though they were every day overcoats. At receptions where the imitation soldiers of Movieland glitter in their imitation uniforms, the imitation bull-fighters wear their gala costumes as if they were the dress clothes of a torero. One should see them at the lunch hour, tea cup and napkin in hand as if they were shaking a cape at the woman with whom they are talking, eating sandwiches with the airs of a banderillero about to place his darts, and raising the cup of champagne as though they were toasting a bull—the bull of the afternoon.

Those metal-covered bull-fighters whose clothes clink as they walk play their rôles even to the point of telling stories of the ring as though they really were toreros.

"Once, in the bull ring in Seville," their tales begin, like those of children, with a homesick "once upon a time."

So daring, so boastful, so swaggering are these movie bull-fighters that they would be quite capable of founding a taurine club and decorating the walls with those bull heads which are sold in the Rag Market, and which always carry a plate engraved with the announcement that this was the bull that killed the famous Espartero. How many bulls are there that killed Espartero? If one could believe those skull plates he must have been attacked by an entire stock farm.

Women think these fake bull-fighters brave men who are capable of anything. So they dash at their gold plated figures with their cameras—those harmless bulls, made safe by the cloth that covers them.

Strangers in Movieland think that all the tassels hung on the gala costume, all the golden buckles and the panels embroidered in gold thread, are decorations awarded to these bull-fighters who have never risked themselves in battle.

"How valiant they are!" a young Englishwoman said once. "They have so many decorations that they cannot find room for them on their breasts, so they distribute them over their bodies and even have clusters of them on their legs."

Those real toreros who are so frightened in front of actual bulls ought to immigrate to the movie country and sign contracts for life promising to march into the bull ring only to the music of gay Movieland fox trots.

Clowns of the bull-fight, they never need be frightened again. Forever afterward they will be happy diplomats representing the bull-fight in the cinema.

Those bull rings of the movies should become a sort of honorable vacation ground for men who have braved great perils, and who may now enter the endless carnival of the movie capital.

Among the fake bull-fighters all is optimism, an optimism as pink as that of rosy stockings, as pink as the color that tinges the plaster image of the infant Jesus sold at fairs in Catholic countries.

When the imitation bull-fighters eventually go to a real fight, they are amazed, and they tell every one who will listen that they have never seen anything so grand.

The paradox of Movieland appears when they go out into the world, for they return converted into such real people that they are no longer of use in the movies.

They have been resurrected, and like all healthy beings, they are of no use to death.

The actor who has a tail-coat which casts a good shadow is in high favor in Movieland.

The actor with a tail-coat shadow is invited to all the parties. In the glass studios he looks like a leader of the orchestra of silence, dressed in the useless garb of suicides.

"What a marvelous shadow his tail-coat casts," every one says in chorus.

His tail-coat is in itself a marvel. It shows no more stitching than if it had been stuck together with glue. In it he seems to have four arms, so expressive are its tails.

"The Shadow Statue" might have been the title of the most characteristic film in his repertoire.

The man with a good tail-coat shadow gives as much distinction to the films in which he appears as though he were a lion of drawing-rooms. Every one is serene while he treads the scenic deck. When he raises his head, with that gesture of taking a smile out of the purse of his soul, he gives every one courage.

The man with a good frock coat evokes conversation with his hands like a juggler, and animates the entire film.

The man with a good tail-coat shadow is the representative of the God of the Movies, his high priest, the master of powerful lights and of the women who serve the temple.

Pawnbroker of hopes of worldliness and elegance, the man with the famous tail-coat and a fine shadow hands out lottery tickets to all who watch him.

There is one Movieland personage who is a visionary, a young person with white hair who is never called on to play anything but apparitions.

He is that being from the past who appears framed in a window which opens at the back of the room just as the hero is about to speak.

He is used for nothing but evoking the emaciated dead.

Thanks to the visionary, all the past is made real, and the film acquires tremendous depth and background.

Subsiding into the past day by day, this old young man is allowed to fade away in the most comfortable fashion.

Half ghost, half human being, like all those who represent visions, his hair a mask of age above a burned and ravaged face, his temples pale as marbles, this man will not live long.

He enjoys great fame in Movieland, for he, who represents a man returning faithfully to the house of his sweetheart, or the young father who died when his son was only two, has thereby become the half-forgotten youth of all of them.

To the comedian he seems lacking in liver or kidneys, breathing through narrow nostrils, languid as an office employee who has rounded out thirty years in the same job, covered with the dust of legal papers, a portrait behind a dusty glass.

Pale, heavy-eyed, like a man so sick he can scarcely breathe in his sleep, he seems to have been flattened between sheets and rendered love-sick by camphor.

CHAPTER XXIX

Carlotta Bray Appears

All Movieland was excited. A marvel had been found. Once again a woman had awakened every one's interest. Like a new star, this apparition had come into sight the previous day, during a nocturnal filming.

They found her working in the middle of the studio. She had chosen her moment and made her entrance. Afterward she confessed that she had been looking through the glass of the Great Studio at the first part of the comedy; it occurred to her to enter the plot. Working as swiftly as a quick-change artist, she put on the proper clothes and make-up, went into the Studio, and was made an unexpected star.

The director, script in hand, was amazed.

That girl had no place in his lines, but she deserved one.

Should he have sounded the whistle to stop all action?

He let that lovely unknown develop for a moment without telling the camera man to cut her life short.

Every one was following the fortunes of a gypsy who had filled the scene with the fascination of her malicious beauty.

Only when he saw that the poor girl was about to break into tears did he blow the whistle which, as with electric cars, stops the endless movie train.

"Pi . . . piii. . . ."

The director approached the woman who had acted as though she were a casual movie artist.

"Who sent you to me? Why are you working here? Who told

you to take part in this film?"

"Mr. Emerson."

"Impossible. You are talking with him now. I could not have forgotten you had I seen you before. Why do you come into the film with emotion enough to kill you? Your chest is heaving like the lid on a boiling kettle."

The girl began to cry.

"Why do you do that," Emerson went on, "when you could become a star without a single tear or a moment's worry?"

The girl was round-eyed with amazement.

Every one took to her as unquestioningly as good Catholics accept the Host at their first communion.

She seemed a child arisen from the waters, a daughter of the sea just come from her mother's arms, so fresh was she, her skin so soft, so faintly humid.

She made a gesture of submissive sorrow, a gesture that was to turn tempestuous only once, on that difficult night when she would be executed against the wall of life.

But every day saw a prelude to that gesture.

Perhaps it was that which attracted every one to her as she stood there solemnly poised above hips too slender for a girl, circled by a cordon of silk.

Carlotta Bray smiled at her admirers in the salons of the Grand Hotel. In her rosy frock she seemed the very blossom of success. Those who, in the full tide of their glory, had not suspected that a rival might arise, saw in her a new proof of the deceitfulness of the movies. She was the seductive one who changed all the fashions, she was the woman whom all lovers sought.

Carlotta Bray held court in the hotel lobby like a millionaire's daughter who has just arrived with a suitcase full of negotiable bonds worth a million dollars.

She had just arrived, but she was already an inspiring figure, the type of young person who owes her success only to herself, and who is hidden behind chain armor. She bore on her breast the scapulary of the chosen one, her own scapulary, the scapulary of the orphan who found Potosi on her own initiative.

She had the perfect purity of the young and new. She smelled as fresh as a newly ironed chemise. She had the clear gaze of a prize winner or of a young god who had ascended to heaven, and escaped from the Calvary which threatened him.

"I am free from you," she seemed to want to say to the obsequious and gallant folk who surrounded her, "and now I can listen to you without fear. Until yesterday the slightest thing would have thrown me back into insignificance."

Carlotta had the green eyes of all the great Carlottas and she knew how to thrust the needle points of her lashes into every one who looked at her.

Between midnight and morning she had become a heroine, but like all true heroines, she knew how to act her part.

"What were you previously?" they asked her.

"Just what I am now," she answered, "for I awaited this with such confidence, I counted on it with such sureness, that it had to be."

"And what gave you that sureness?" they asked.

"I am the type that represents the girls of my day," she answered. "Therefore I have hastened, lest I should lose the chance of being their heroine."

"But what axiom of art moved you?"

"That there must be one eye which weeps and another which smiles, and I have those two different eyes and those two poles of character."

Carlotta offered every one the hope of her body, which she kept as it had been when her mother had washed it with soft sponges.

Seated in a great chair, her left forearm lying across the right, as if it were a balustrade, she let her cigarette hand hang idly, and provocatively.

All the young feminine leadership of the world awoke in this sixteen-year-old girl.

The world wove webs of hope for itself and tried to persuade itself it could trap her.

A new war began. Every one around her became stubborn.

The desire of perverting innocence, of hearing all over again how strange those things seem which the world has experienced to the point of satiety—this always fascinates men.

By now this girl who looked like a beautiful beggar was insured for millions of dollars.

Yesterday they would not have given a cent for her.

But she is a wayward, valiant, daring creature.

All Movieland bows around her, and in the strange cohort of different types even the famous fox-terrier, insured by a huge policy, who looks upon the whole world with great indifference, looks at her with eager and desirous eyes.

CHAPTER XXX

Carlotta Under the Violet Lights

All the apparatus of the Great Studio assumed an added interest when it lent itself to the long-limbed girl with thighs like a schoolboy's.

Day and night they made the most out of this new ingenue. She was going to move the world, and they hurried to take advantage of her charm lest she fall victim to the flu or to a competitor.

The casts passed in single file before an inspector who gave a final touch to wigs here, sewed up a hole there, looked them over as customs officers do baggage.

In the great Zeppelin hangar which is the movie pavilion, there is a brilliant dawn.

In the hall of human machines the drama of moving pictures gets under way.

As the month of August in Movieland is extremely hot, the whole studio is plunged in ice like a bottle of champagne before it is served.

The paths and doors which lead to the studio are full of "No Admittance" signs pointing in that lion-like gesture with which one throws a person out of the house.

That "No Admittance" is impressed on every one's spirit. Before so many "No Admittance" signs the world is plunged in timidity.

Many people, appalled at so much "No Admittance," flee and never come back.

The huge movie station sends forth reels of film as a railroad station sends out an endless tail of trains.

The tin cans of light shine gorgeously.

It seems as though all the automobiles congregated in that spot are focussing their lights on a single point.

Within there sounds a voice, dry, brutal as an auto horn, which shouts: "Camera."

Silence rules in the room. Spectators who find it almost impossible to be still take out handkerchiefs and stuff them in to impose silence on their mouths.

One hears only the formidable eloquence of light, and that sound like the humming of white butterflies which is the sputtering of carbons.

The magnesium reserves of the world are lighted. For some time it will not be possible to take a portrait or photograph the arrival of a celebrity in all the world.

The pantomime is utterly serious.

Those searchlights which chased the rum runners out the door and lit up the margins of the sea seek for the other characters.

The Director with his heavy megaphone makes one smile, for the scene looks like a familiar childish game in which youngsters seize the horn of a phonograph and invent voices—the voice of savage ogres, the voice of a dark cavern, a presumptuous voice.

The Director of that scene yells like a raucous phonograph:

"Hug her hard!"

"Now, a passionate kiss!"

"Now strangle her!"

"Harder, harder!"

"Let her fall on the ground!"

The voice of the Director makes a tyrant out of him.

The Director's way of seeing is called super-vision. So he sits proudly in a canvas chair, like a strategist meditating on a victorious battle.

"Fool, fool, that wink. Her dress ought to fall off her shoulder at the same time. A wink is not a gesture. It whispers of a dimly lighted secret boudoir. The closing of the eye urges the man winked at toward that boudoir. You understand?"

The celebrity bathes on the movie beach.

Her jewels are imitation, for it had been proven that real gems are too dull under the artificial lights of the cinema.

Rouged mummies remind one of Egyptian mummies whose faces were hardened by oils. Some of their faces seem to be made of cardboard.

Carlotta, who had attracted that part of the public which goes to the most important festivals, was sublime.

She presented a lie full of seriousness. She was the woman whose word cannot be doubted, yet she was creating the greatest lie in the world, the lie which is a film.

Her acting seemed truth itself. She made gestures as if guarding the kisses and caresses in her very heart.

That woman was not an actress. She was woman, true and sincere, with arms made for loving and beauty that was royal and austere.

Woman is content with the mute art of the films. She does not have to justify her acts except by gestures. She likes to chatter but she does not wish to justify with beautiful words what she does from moment to moment.

She distracted every one who worked with her. It was difficult to make sure that the action revolved about her and at the same time keep every one from staring at her.

Elsa walked out like a queen, but she was a queen who had lost her throne and who heard in her ears the wails of the exiled.

Elsa was the only one who did not seek her dressing room. As befitted the Queen of Movieland, she had had a tiny cottage built for movie bathing in a corner of the gleaming studio beach. That tent in the midst of the great movie encampment, fitted into one corner like a secret lamp attached to the most enormous of wires, gave Elsa great independence. It saved her from the necessity of bathing directly before the film in order to enter with that ideal freshness demanded of her.

Afterward Virginia left.

Virginia disclosed the secret of that swan-like grace which characterized her, a secret of which the public who watched her had no knowledge.

An orchestra led by a violin was the thing which gave to the romantic Virginia that sentimental air which made her so alluring. Invisible music, music unsuspected by her audiences, moved her to those subtle and delicate gestures, made her weep those tears which welled not from tear ducts but up from the bottom of her soul.

That music was the track on which her poetic grace moved. A rhythm which was never heard gave atmosphere to her entire rôle.

From time to time every one plunged his eyes into blue eye cups. The mercury lamps burned them more fiercely than the light of the desert.

All of them had lost their lashes, and taken to wearing artificial ones. They were all afraid of Kleig eyes, a horrid illness produced by the Kleig lamps.

Blue eyes came out of their adrenaline bath bluer than ever. But the salts in the light made them smart again, and seek the watery comfort of the tiny eye cups.

Again the cranks of the recording cameras took up their eternal grinding.

Even after it had ceased the noise of the cranks stayed in every one's ears. They could never forget it. It was engraved on their very ear drums.

Neither could they forget their death-like appearance under

the violet lights. Looking as though decomposition had already begun, they were at the same time galvanized into more vigorous life by that electric emotion.

A god, who lit the studio with mercury vapor, was present at the spectacle. In the movies the god of all is a god who improvises, a god given to making ephemeral worlds and souls which even at the moment of being do not exist.

A god without punishment, for how can he create punishments for those imitation crimes whose end is known before the film is finished?

Carlotta was expected again, and when she reappeared, a group of unknown spectators, who had managed to bribe every Cerberus that guarded the gates, burst forth and swarmed on all the railings, above the lamps, everywhere.

During the recess the room was filled with the charm of a lovely girl who for the first time was discovering for herself the secrets of her body.

The Director watched her at close range, seeing her gestures increase, noting how she unfolded a new tide of Spring to the eager gaze of the world. Before the powerful thrusts of that swimmer the very spaces awoke.

The glory of the screen shone beneath the great light of the movie hangar, like one of those aureoled virgins which appear in natural grottoes.

The scenario writer threw away his script and even let her invent things which occurred to her. She fell into those attitudes of the ideal beggar maid which suggested a new sketch.

CHAPTER XXXI

Max Breaks with Elsa

IN THE DINING-ROOM the light filtered through lace curtains; the world famous beauty rested in her rocking chair. It was hot in Movieland. Elsa wore only a dressing gown, but it was a poem of a gown, as lovely as a white mantilla.

The palms in the dining-room shone fresh and untouched like a plate of salad which is never seasoned and eaten, but kept as part of the ritual of the dining-room.

The homely white filter was like a water clock dripping off the minutes of a siesta.

Elsa, who had a dull headache, called the maid who attended her in intimate hours when she did not like the other servants near her.

"Marga, stop the filter."

Marga looked at her in amazement. Her mistress had given the order as simply as though she had said, "Stop the clock." But could one stop a filter as easily as a clock?

Elsa noticed her confusion and said, "Take it inside where I can't hear its eternal dripping."

Marga lifted the fresh supply of patient water, and disappeared with it; it was still murmurous, forever whispering intimate confessions.

A monotonous summer day, made worse by disillusion, took its slow way down the afternoon.

All the windows had closed their eyelids. It was as though blinds had been drawn on show windows full of cakes and candies.

In the withdrawal of the houses there was something of the sweet and dazzling whiteness of cocoanut and sugar.

All the shadows had fled. The very lintels of the doorways had no eyebrows.

Through the broad windows of second story rooms came an atmosphere of hair dressing shops and dentists offices.

Everything was a ghost in a piqué frock.

Those who sat behind window shades and curtains seemed to be wearing the white garments of brides. It looked as though there were a great many of them and probably there was not a single one.

Every one lay in the depths of divans, drugged with languor, slippers flung into the farthest corners.

Max seethed with the impatience of a man who cannot resist the woman beside him, yet is furious because "everything is over" and everything bothers him.

The mutual recrimination which is brewed in summer dining-rooms was brewing in that one.

The memory of Carlotta as queen of the festival floated in air that was heavy with the afternoon's sleep.

That morning Max had arisen in despair, full of a disgust he had caught from some dream. It was the kind of dream which marks the end of a stage on life's journey.

He stumbled over Elsa's shoes, which were scattered about the room. Furious, maddened by that profusion of shoes, he had asserted that she had a hundred and eighty pairs. He said, "Look here, your shoes have the same effect on me as a nest of rats. The white ones rule, the black ones slink out of sight. I'm disgusted with so many shoes."

Elsa sat up in bed. She had detected the first sign of aversion in Max's words. A woman knows when she hears the first signs of the end of love. That he had been annoyed by stumbling over her shoes gave her the key to what was going on in his mind.

Everything was over that morning, but there had to be a scene that afternoon. On what pretext?

On the shelves of the console table and the sideboard there stood certain jars decorated with rosy ribbons.

"You never will throw away those pink bows. 1 can not stay here a minute longer unless you let me take the ribbons off those jars."

"No, no!" she cried, as though they were threatening her with death, or as though they wanted to remove the hair ribbons from the two small nieces she had adorned, and whose weeping appalled her.

Elsa's attack of nerves was as long as a farewell, and a farewell it undoubtedly was.

She was already feeling like a blown-out fuse compared to that restless youngster who symbolized the new virgin. This is the way the passions of men as corrupt and scheming as Max are revived.

CHAPTER XXXII

Carlotta and Every One

CARLOTTA PUT INTO THE FILMS all the joy and the high spirits of the new leaders of the world.

Thanks to Carlotta, captious movie houses had become theaters full of devotees. New gestures of laughter and coquetry awoke in her.

She already had the terrible obstinacy of one who is to choose the perfect man. She was the youngster for whom distant deeds of violence were committed, deeds which sent those who committed them to jail where they wore the pyjamas of the insomniac for fifteen or twenty years.

How a youngster can fill a whole town with her grandeur, for they follow her like a queen only to see her ivory bracelets on her rosy arm.

Her ingenuous way of rejecting a convenient phrase, only to pick it up later in sudden agreement, gave her a supernatural charm.

Her tender beauty increased the desire hidden in every one to make her lose the innocence of which she was not yet aware.

That is the thing to which the world comes back again and again. There is always new innocence to be perverted, innocence which bears no relation to that already ruined, innocence which is primordial and absolute merely because it is the latest.

All the ardor of Movieland was concentrated on Carlotta. Exquisite and an artist, she was able to invoke thousands of lovely innocents with her own innocence.

The public was as absorbed in her as was Movieland. The theaters went on dreaming of her after her pictures were over. No one took out a newspaper to read between acts.

Seated at every one's side, she became a bare-armed girl who quite without malice tilted one eye at every one in a fatal wink.

Every one pursued her, but the most annoying were those gymnastic people whose strong hands sought to shake her arms so as to produce a ripple in her firm breasts. They shook hands as though they were throwing a stone in a lake and poring over its concentric circles.

She, like a skilled cyclist, swift, agile, brooking no interference, passed through their midst.

She wore a skirt belted at the hips like the fringed leather chaps of those who ride wild horses.

Only Theodore Bonvel kept watch over her.

Theodore Bonvel loved her. He had been her father in a film and since then he had loved her like a father. She called him father, anxious for his protection, as in that long movie in which she was snatched from the fury of a bear by Theodore's knife.

Theodore Bonvel did not believe in sons. Those women to whom he had been a casual husband, and who usually had a daughter of whom they were very fond, heard him say, "I wish it had been a son so you could see me eat him."

Even the dwarf made love to Carlotta, finding courage in his deformity.

The fox-terrier looked at her with eyes burning like live coals, begging the caress which sends even dogs into ecstasies of trembling.

Carlotta, proud as an animal trainer entering the cage of her wild beasts, dined and laughed with her adorers in the freest fashion, completely uncontaminated, given to the most absurd desires. One of these was for sardines' brains at wholesale, and in this she exceeded the desire of many women for fried sardine brains at retail, an ideal held by many women but difficult to satisfy in quantity.

Spent men fastened burning eyes on Carlotta's gracious ones.

Even the Director joined in the pursuit of Carlotta, and his crocodile skin became soft and supple.

Where the Director had paid court he had always won, but with Carlotta he was not so fortunate. One could see him sniff the perfume of her curved body, of those unhampered breasts, firm and smooth and polished as only free breasts are.

The Director knew how to keep his devouring passion in check. He hid it well. One saw it only in the way he smoked cigarettes, inhaling them with such violence that he reduced them to ashes in a single puff.

And Carlotta took her gay way through the midst of everything. Bobbed haired and intrepid, she was like a new Pandora holding a box full of the secret of the world, laughing with the grace of one who does not know and does not suspect what evil it may contain.

Carlotta, seeing everything through mists of illusion, felt unreal and insecure, a voyager who travels to places which do not exist. She did not want to lose the way.

She did not wish for the black and blue marks which are men's sign and seal on the white arms of women.

She had already bought a tiger cub to play with on week-ends, and every morning she wore the white garb ordained for Sunday. Some of her suitors went so far as to insult her in order to stir up her pride.

"You are as unconsciously gay as a parasol."

"You are just a bunch of paper flowers. There is no heart in you, no perfume, nor even the echo of a bird song."

"You are a tiny shadow on a wall—nothing more."

Carlotta, impassive, defended her fragile self like those young and beautiful women who seem so strangely out of place in lion houses. They stir up the lions merely by passing in front of their cages, yet they are safe from a single scratch.

Gay, young and beautiful, a country girl in the world's lion house, Carlotta had no other wish than to be a peaceful tourist on this earth. She never wanted to tear from her eyes the veils which are kind to imperfections.

All men would have given anything they possessed to shower her with whatever was necessary that they might know her vision, dim her life, rid her of the girlish gayety that kept her laughing. She played like a child in the clear afternoon of the best human zoo in the world. The zoo that is Movieland.

CHAPTER XXXIII

The Censor

EVERY ONE HUNG BREATHLESS on the action of the censor. Would the censor allow such scandalous beauty to slip its lithe seduction through the films?

The pictures in which Carlotta appeared were not passionate, but their effect was the same as though they had been.

She feared the censor's first glimpse of her in the black art of the movies. How terrible to have the censor write with a hatpin on the frightened celluloid: "Absolutely shocking!"

The distant censor cuts the best out of the pictures.

The censors, sordid, and dressed in black, elbow each other meaningly. In the dark projection room of the censorship board, they cut the best part out of the film, the gayest and the clearest.

The censor's projection room when light announces an intermission is enough to frighten the bravest.

The old maids distribute themselves among the boxes, each wearing a rusty and militant black hat. Those ladies had descended from coaches so old they smelled of moth balls.

They had committed the unspeakable sin. Ordering ices served to them in an open coach, they lapped them up like old black cats, or rather, like cats which are half black and half white. The whole street marveled at the greediness of old age.

A line of coaches, of the kind that usually go to funerals, stood patiently outside the hypocritical offices of the censorship board.

If the movie artists could only see that room. But it is fortunate that they cannot, for it would terrify them so that they could not work.

All the women wore lace mitts, and looked like crows perched on the railings of boxes.

They had a dry nervous cough and they carried huge and hypocritical fans composed of much paper and short ribs, fans with which they could cover their eyes at difficult moments and yet peek between the ribs.

Two whalebones in each collar kept their heads firmly upright.

Their collar bones showed through the yokes of black gauze dotted with lying beauty marks.

They were the mistresses of servants who were worked to death, and their grandsons were those children of caricature who always seem sea-going geese on their way to mass.

Usually they were deaf, and so their eyes bulged like binoculars as they looked about them with the uncertain glance of the deaf.

Arms pressed close against their hips they watched the film in offended silence.

The men who accompanied them a pace in the rear looked as though they were making a visit of condolence in which some one was guilty of an indiscretion. It was as though a widow should die of laughter as she was talking with her next lover.

When the light went on in the room at the end of the guilty film, some of the men had their eyes bandaged with handkerchiefs as heavily bordered with black as though they were silken death notices. Their wives had bound them when the immorality was at its height.

Many of them carried the misty monocle of censorship, which they cleaned with black-edged mourning handkerchiefs during the intermissions.

The nervous film, trembling more than ever, disclosed its shielded sun. In it there was the laughter of a world one reaches on tourist trains. Men off pictures post cards passed by, leaving the country as empty as though all the pigeons had flown to the great plazas of St. Mark.

The censors, restless in their seats, waited like the policemen and the witnesses called by the judge to give evidence against a married man.

Everything happened in the film as it does in the wide world of those who leap into an automobile to go off and lose themselves in an empty corner.

At moments during the immoral film, a black glove would slap against the white curtain, and when light went on it became apparent that they were mitts which had been thrown from horny, grasping fingers.

The smiling film passed by, its gayety posed against a background of cloud and sunshine.

In the projection room there were many comments.

"Did you see that woman smoking? Can't have that."

"Ah!" It was the cry of a saint about to faint and needing smelling salts. "She and he in pyjamas in the same boudoir."

The film, which was as respectable as life, grew smaller and smaller before the censors' notes. Tiny flashlights lit the pads on which they jotted down prohibitions, observations, cuts.

The film, which had no idea of what was going to happen to it, unrolled its frank and slangy length, shot through with long moments of light in which it seemed to open its eyes too wide. Only after the picture was over did the congress meet in the assembly hall.

"The kiss in the second part lingers like a fever sore. It is positively wicked."

"That is true. We will at least have to make it shorter."

"Yes. Let them take five seconds off it," ordered the Director.

The order went down on paper.

"And the hug in the fourth part?"

"Impossible. We have ordered that all hugs last no more than a yard of film, nor less than two seconds."

In the censors' black art there is full revenge against Movieland.

The middle-class outside of Movieland had to endure the fact that their jurisdiction did not reach that corner of the world. They had to stand by silently while the free film people mocked at their middle-class manners. Matters were not improved by the fact that the deepest irony lay in the lives they led when they were completely free.

From their frontiers of lazy light the movie people laughed at all the families that set middle-class snares in dark places. At times they seemed to smile at the egotism which they stirred up without having the slightest faith in it.

On the screen they portrayed a life which was anachronistic and funny to them, but sometimes they went a bit too far and then the censor took vengeance.

That was why the censors carried on such a bitter discussion in the case of Carlotta Bray, the most alluring girl in all the world. One single kiss of hers, light and quick though it might be, awoke a mad desire for kisses through the whole theater. The consumption of caramels increased to such an extent that at the end of one of her films all the automatic caramel vendors on the backs of seats were empty.

How could the censors justify a decision against the ideal girl who flashed her smiles across every curtain?

They found no way. Moreover, the men who were censorship judges wanted to bask again and again in the glow of that woman's smiles, and if a picture is judged wicked, the censors unfortunately cannot run it over again, much less acquire the most vivid ones for themselves as does Mayor Gorton, that energetic and implacable member of the Council of Censors.

CHAPTER XXXIV

The Academy of Kisses

When Elsa realized she had been abandoned, she began to plot ways of vengeance against that fickle and fatuous man who was running after the girl who was at once a new movie butterfly and a little angel in gorgeous garters.

To put a lighted hand over her door would have annoyed her. Should she hunt another virile movie figure? She was fed up with fatuous men.

Then she ordered a huge electric sign made on which were the words:

ACADEMY OF KISSING
FOR
MEN AND WOMEN
Professor Elsa Broters

The sign was lighted, to the scandal of Movieland and to the annoyance of Max. Immediately the whole great public of extras who aspire to be stars applied for instruction.

Elsa enjoyed bringing her pupils' kisses together, and she made the strangest combinations. Her drawing-room was charged with a kind of emotional electricity after so many kisses. The computing of their numbers went into the realm of higher mathematics.

Like blackboards full of words and formulæ, the wall panels were covered with the imprint of nervous, trembling kisses.

Pressed on at all angles, the kisses were scattered as thick as those golden bees which were stamped on old imperial papers.

All those free and eager young things had given their first kisses in utter good faith, but not one of the first kisses reached the point of perfection which could only be attained by the last. It was a long search.

There were youths who stood with their lips parted, completely exhausted, almost pulseless, unable to strike the note of a convincing kiss, a kiss which should not seem that of a wet-nurse on Elsa's broad mirrors.

Repelled by the kisses that were given them, almost all the girls, in their anxiety for one of those luminous kisses that raises a film to the realm of the immortal, kissed and kissed unceasingly. They were drunk on kisses, as each kiss went to lose itself in the interminable series of those already given.

The search for the deep chest "do" which prevails in an academy of song had its equivalent in that academy of the kiss in an attempt to find the osculatory "do" in the kissing duet of movie practice.

"A kiss," that wise and experienced woman explained, "is first a thing for which a woman reaches, and last the thing with which she bids farewell. You must not forget this. Never give an absent-minded kiss, an insipid or submissive one, never give a kiss that lacks suggestion."

Every one listened to her without thinking of inventing a real kiss. They were fascinated by the falsest kisses in the world.

"The kiss," that woman continued, eloquent as a mystic in whose ear the white dove speaks, "is the only relaxation of the soul, the only moment in which the soul breathes outside itself, like those fishes which for a single instant thrust their mouths out of the water. The kiss should stamp its burning self on the lips as leather workers press their golden flowers into ruddy leather. The kiss, my dear pupils, is a carnation which is born, and flaunts its fluted edges, never to be born again."

Her reputation as a distinguished woman whose kisses inspired respect in the very kissing bugs themselves, kept her classes from degenerating into something beyond kissing contests. The complexions of her women students grew soft as the skin of a peach.

How one judges the worth of one man compared with another is the way he knows how to kiss!

In those tiny rooms there were charming kissing parties, and just as one ordinarily moves from one conversation to another, so there one moved from one kiss to another, without having to make any declarations or claims of merit-meeting the spontaneous richness of certain lips or the friendly mother-of-pearl of a cheek without any of the bitter harshness of opposition.

"There is no language as universal as that of kisses," said the beautiful professor. "You may laugh at Esperanto. Neither the loveliest phrase nor the most beautiful silence can be compared to a good kiss, although in order to achieve one you must have men who cleanse their teeth of tartar and their souls of egotistic passions."

Later she explained embraces. "In embracing, one is a doctor who listens for the slightest sound that he may make a diagnosis. Embraces of that sort are the most mysterious and the ones which impress a woman most. Make her think that you are meditating over her, that you are seeking the secret of her heart. No brusque gymnast's embraces, nor quick dashes as of a waiter trying to make the most of a moment behind the pantry door. Gather her into your arms slowly, even though you miss your train."

In the exchange of kissing every one hunted the mouth which was best suited to his own. It is not enough to have the finest kissing lips and the greatest skill. It is also necessary that the lips you seek be good and favorable.

In the lesson on "Negro Kisses," Elsa was at her best, for

she dragged up to the platform poor Simpson, who had always adored her, and who had already gained fame as the one who stayed after classes to hunt like a big black dog under the furniture for any pupil who might have fallen by the wayside.

"We must," said Elsa, "accept the kisses of these men who seem to have arisen out of hell or from the depths of some dark well solely through the desire for white kisses. We should not cut those kisses short. We must give them time. They are kisses which eat us up, for at heart they are the kisses of cannibals."

After expounding the theory of negro kisses she called Simpson. Trembling as he came toward her, he took her in his arms as though she were the virgin of his dreams, and on her cheeks he printed the rubber stamp of his lips. The thick-lipped kisses of the negro were unusually slow. His mouth seemed full of them.

Bit by bit the class grouped itself into couples for the best kissing. These were the favorites of the teacher, and the leaders of the class.

In practice lessons, Elsa, anxious to offend Max with all those kisses, caught at her youthful pupils as though they were the branches of a cherry tree, and devoured their kisses with a hunger that astonished all her students.

Afterward she let them kiss her so that the girls might see how a woman must give herself up to a kiss, making of herself the living wine, that the kiss may have about it something of a first communion.

It pleased Elsa to wear her garment of kisses like a robe of pearls. They rustled as she moved, and their light sound was a derisive whisper in the ear of him who had dared to make her jealous of Carlotta, whose kisses might be fresh and adolescent, but lacked the subtlety of hers.

CHAPTER XXXV

News Reel. Films in the Country.
Handsome Men and Homely Ones.
Virginia Pregnant. The Gland Robbers.

MOVIELAND SHOOK with ceaseless grinding out of films. The world demanded more every day. The sad proletariat felt the necessity of filling its long vacation with shadows.

Every one feared that television would hatch out in some hidden corner as the enemy of those long strips of celluloid that were sent forth in such great numbers. Everything might be changed in the future, for projection might be made by radio.

The contract made with Baby Tommy ran for three years, because after that he would be a grown boy bearing only the terrible traces of his exploited babyhood in a barbarous gesture, or a gigantic and dreadful tear.

He was interned in Movieland with a fabulous sum, but as soon as he reached adolescence he would be thrown out with loathing for his past childhood. He would be a good-looking boy, with strongly modeled nostrils and guarded eyes set deep in their orbits.

Movieland's craze for showing off was appalling. They even added the famous Duomo with its lacy shadow to the town.

Why go to Milan to see the Duomo? They were just cynical enough to disdain the real and admire their imitation.

It was not going to last more than fifteen days, but it had the proportions and the modeling of the real one. The haughty people who were the owners of the real Duomo could do nothing but endure the monotony of their famous monument, while the dwellers in Movieland would change about from place to place and vary their buildings to suit themselves.

The most beautiful pagoda of Japan, the very Duomo of pagodas, had left its shadow there like a victim fallen on the great scaffold of monuments.

The operators worked day and night, bent over their machines like motor cyclists always in leather leggings, always deft of arm and absorbed of face, for they knew that their machines would catch and record everything.

They were always taking measurements with the compass-like legs of thin tripods, always driving their long claws into the ground, making camp, and setting up the machines in automobile trucks, in airplanes, even in locomotives, taking advantage of the slope of the machine, the platform at the top of its triangulated legs, the shelf which protected them against the vibration threatening the machine in the speeding train.

They made the train, ponderous as a mastodon, stop wherever they wished, for the track of that Movieland train went nowhere and stopped at no city where they would be molested by notaries and consuls.

The operators in their webbing caps had forgotten how to walk except with their three-legged cane, a mysterious cane in which the photographic tripod hides.

They cannot get along without the aid of their tripod. Long-nailed, it seems a staff rather than a cane. In the midst of the fields they look like employees of the Federal Tax Commission about to punish the inhabitants by raising their taxes.

Mornings became more and more popular. The breakfast of working days was a marvelous meal which the restaurants served *à la carte*.

"Every seven o'clock lobster left the sea at dawn. At 7 A. M. all sea food is ideal. It bears the flavor of the first day of creation."

They had to find ways of compensating for the necessity of working in the morning; it is the most dreadful thing about the profession.

How they hoped for the sun at times, every one watching the sky as hopefully as if he were a mystic praying to God!

The most difficult mornings were those which had a country feeling to them, which made one realize he was in the fields of God, the fields of farmers and fruit growers. Then they knew the horrid paradox of being caught in the greatest farce of being pursued by nature while working at the most artificial art in the world in the midst of nature's incredulous laughter.

Falsifying a thing in a set was a very different matter from doing it in the open country.

Tons of salt imitated snow. All the salt cellars of the world showered down on the chosen spot, a trick which the spectator could not discover as he could not stick a wet finger into the salt.

White woolen costumes, long skis, spiked staffs, and thick woolen gloves all helped to make the sensation complete. Even the sudden spells of heat seemed spells of cold.

But the thing which inflicted on the morning a wound no sticking plaster could cure was the enormous prompter's mirror. It reflected the bland indifference of the sky to all their words, and showed it clear and cloudless when they were most haggard and sleepy-eyed.

Only Carlotta was fresh enough to face the morning. She filled it with all the interest that attends on competition, she even flirted with the sun, sending it winks and smiles which made the hour endurable.

Young and lively, she gave such added interest to the morning that as numerous a public came to see the spectacle of its dawning as though she were christening a new battleship.

Handsome men took immediate refuge in Movieland. These handsome men were the failures of the world. They did not understand the rest of mankind.

Their problems as handsome men demanded special solution and much money. They did not understand the world at all. Being nobodies, they tried to be somebody in Movieland, which is the one place where only a vivid person can become a world-famous personage. Those of the handsome men who managed to become known thought themselves cocks of the walk with a great future before them, cocks who had arrived, cocks elevated to the bird museum in the human chicken house.

All of them felt themselves made men for the rest of their lives, stars who would outlast the centuries.

They avoided all contact with careers, all military duty and jury service. They were interested only in that eternal tennis game which is the cinema.

In the city club they regarded the future with patronizing disapproval.

Along with the handsome men there went the homely men of Movieland, who tried to make a joke of their ugliness.

All the Quasimodos in the world eaten by their appalling ugliness wanted to preen themselves on the sets and regale the world with their grimaces.

Director Emerson was tired of receiving them. During his years of reviewing ugliness he had learned the trick of turning his eyes inward, and he always took refuge in that when too many of them came to ask for screen tests.

But the homeliest man any one remembered in Movieland was so full of tumors, so swollen with elephantiasis, that the day after he was admitted he had an operation and died without ever getting onto the screen.

Virginia, sweet Virginia who had recently shown Movieland

such a charming example of disinterested and ingenuous love, was filling out.

As soon as Director Emerson found out that Virginia was really growing large, and that it was not, as he had believed, merely the way she wore her corset, he called the actress and made a violent scene.

"So it is a son?"

"Or a daughter. One can't be sure of anything yet."

"Good. I'm not interested in its sex. The important thing is that this cannot go on. We have certain very important plans on hand which need your figure. This thing is impossible. Your contract forbids it."

"It is all the more movie-like—to be pregnant!"

"This is not a joke. It is more likely to ruin us—all of us. Virginia Cooper the great actress cannot have a child. It is the last straw. It is indecent, this swelling. It is like a boil, a tumor, an accretion of pus. No, we cannot allow this here."

"An accretion of pus? And every one that is born? What are you yourself?"

"I was that accretion of pus growing in an unlucky woman and it cost me a great deal to save myself from that condition to which most beings yield. A son above all is a dreadful thing. I am master here, and sorry as I am, you must pack up and leave with the man who led you astray. The child must be born elsewhere. A pretty silhouette you would make on the screen!"

After that the Director issued certain orders and Virginia and her lover left Movieland.

The crimes of Movieland were fantastic. There were constant thefts of glands by the "gland robbers" who imitated the feats of the famous brothers.

There gland robbers, voracious, impassive, without the slightest sense of obligation to their position or their epoch, exemplified in their hunger for glands the exalted idea which our age has of glands, and above all for those glands which it is the saddest to lose.

To the gland robbers, every man was rich and powerful, and carried within himself the secret of his fortune. Even the poorest, if he was young, possessed in his glands a fabulous amount of wealth. A capital composed of neither gold nor diamonds, it was white, crude, with a most pressing carnal appetite.

The gland robbers operated in the forests which surround Movieland. They left men useless, and suddenly meek, possessed of a most grievous injury and bemoaning the loss of a priceless treasure.

Thanks to rapid negotiations on the part of the gland robbers, old men in secret corners regained their youth and paid a golden price for its recovery.

CHAPTER XXXVI

On the Artificial Island

THAT ISLAND CONCOCTED off the coast of Movieland and valued at so many millions has been turned into a pleasure ground for people who want to lose themselves.

There was no particular mystery about it, but the island did not appear on maritime charts. The very sea itself shivered with jealousy on touching it. The waves that dashed impetuously on the nearby beaches fell silent as they approached that island, and threw themselves on the ground before it like well-trained horses kneeling in salute.

The fear of tradition which weighs heavily on real islands had no effect here. It was a new island. For its anchoring, great chunks of cement armed against the tireless waters had been given to the sea.

The trees, the flowers, the cottages which covered the fertile surface of the island had all been carried over from the mainland.

It was completely outside any jurisdiction, for it was sufficiently separated from the coast to be apart from the great city which ruled all Movieland.

The artificial island eluded even the jurisdiction of Director Emerson. It was so big that the films which needed so many zigzag roads for their unwinding would be run there easily.

There was no solitude more absurd than that of the imitation island. It was a perfect island for robots. The world took it as a joke, though the new spirit waxed strong there.

There the movie poets felt themselves inspired, and those who were exhausted replenished their forces. The ones who had run out of titles uncovered fresh veins of picturesque new titles which would leave a novel suggested but still invisible.

Unknown animals appeared there which the naturalists themselves could not place, and among the spontaneous flora there were such strange species as the pure movie blossom, the wild flower of the films which shines with a luminous white radiance in the midst of the island night. They simulated those cracks and scratchings which shine like beams on the gray film.

They did not want to list this invented island in the registry of islands lest people laugh at it.

Meanwhile the island upheld its own truth with considerable courage. Its roots went deeper and deeper, as if submarine cables had fastened it to the bottom of the sea.

The imitation island, which geologists and archaeologists of the future were to dower with a most marvelous and ancient history, was like the transatlantic island whose hotels attract many guests who come on the biggest ocean liners.

All the hopes of Carlotta's suitors were centered on taking her to the island, but she heard its marvels recounted without deciding to go.

She would not go unless some film made it necessary.

Every one hoped to win her on the day when he should take her to the island to dine.

But at last, feeling very brave and not wishing to seem a coward in her victory over love, she decided one night to go with her most insistent suitor, August Morel, who believed quite firmly that he could break down her will.

The night was a perfect night for the sea. All its waves seemed to lead a relaxed and lazy life of their own.

"But, Carlotta, what reason have you for not falling in love?"

"All those which give me peace and make me happy."

"But will you never give in?"

"Perhaps some time, but always knowing what a fake it is."

"And on a night like this you feel no love?"

"Of course I do, but I am in love with the night, with the hope of something which, if it happens, must come slowly. The thing I do not want is to distract my attention from the marvelous balance which with the night is poised above us."

It was clear that this supper which had lacked for nothing was going to lack love. The only hope of that intrepid man sped away like moments spent on a railway platform.

The beautiful girl who was so close seemed to be so very far away. The desire of possessing her kindled this contrast into flame.

She was so very near, and yet so very far away.

The island was demoralizing. Utterly without law or government, it spurred August on to further struggles.

She laughed even as she refused herself to him; she laughed and made a joke of the feathery spray of desire.

There began a struggle whose ending was unknown. The sea whispered dreamy and scandalous tales around the island. The stars in their various courses played the jazz band of their differences. The moon was a trap drum.

She herself grew almost afraid. It was not his desire alone that she feared, but the desire of all that nature which urged him on and was speaking through him.

They were roused out of themselves by the terrible shrieks of people caught in a wreck.

In the sudden shock of fear they forgot their own emotions and rushed down to the shore.

It was a shipwreck with many victims, some of them injured in the side, if one could judge by their gestures, others whose screams held the dread rattle of death.

How could the artificial island respond to that call for help?

The waiters at the hotel hurled the tables into the sea to act as life-rafts for the shipwrecked. There were no life savers there.

"The doors! Tear off all the wooden doors and throw them in!" cried the hotel proprietor.

Carlotta under the waning moon appeared like the Virginal Carmen on high in a picture of hell. Instead of the flames of fire there were the flames of life tossing in the furious sea.

They stretched out their hands to her without knowing who she was, heartened by the beauty which some of them remembered as a thing seen in some far away vision.

The ship, impaled on the imitation rocks of the coast, seemed to have thrust up its prow to act as a pulpit for the funeral services over the wreck, that it might be something more than mere man who appeared on that point.

Threatening the shipwrecked with the claws of its greedy waves, the sea seemed to be making the most of its opportunity.

Towering and broken, it had certain film characteristics which the experienced movie star recognized as belonging to no known picture. It was horrible.

August himself was filled with a sudden respect for Carlotta. He understood what consolation there was in the sight of her austere beauty, and he was moved at having been able to take that comforting vision to those who drowned almost within reach of it.

"Help us!"

"Help!"

And the victims had to wait for a hand which should lift them out of their fatal plight.

The power of her beauty gave an illusion of hope. "What island is this?" a man asked the couple. Battered, wet, he held a pistol in one hand like a movie actor in the moment of tragedy.

"The artificial island of the movies," Carlotta answered.

"What? The artificial island of the movies?"

"Yes. The island that was made for 'Horrors of the Sea.'"

The dramatic man with his braided trousers made an indefinable gesture of scorn and sarcasm, and throwing his pistol away, exclaimed, "Ah, then I cannot commit suicide. How simple!"

The thing which takes away some of the horror of the shipwreck and at the same time makes it worse, is the fact that the screams of its victims do not go on forever. In this absurd catastrophe the victims were extinguished one by one, like candles, and the silence of death stole over the sea.

Both of them glowed with the warm feeling that they had granted a great favor to so many lives. It was all because on a certain moonlit night they had wished to celebrate the defeat of love on an island so solitary that it can be marked on the charts of the sea by no degree of latitude and longitude.

CHAPTER XXXVII

A Wedding Followed by a Divorce

The Director of Movieland appeared in his office after his morning shower bath of eau de cologne. His eyes, just opened, were bordered with flat black Japanese rims. He gave close attention to his finger nails, and then to the tops of his shoes. There seemed to be some unknown connection between them. The Director's most elegant servant, who had about him more of the movie theater than of the palace, announced the day's first caller.

"Miss Carlotta Bray is in the salon."

On hearing this, Director Emerson started violently. So, Carlotta was there.

He went to her in the salon. She was making the most of the moment of waiting by comparing herself with a haughty statue.

She staked her own high pride against the statue and defied its beauty with her own.

The Director went straight to the heart of the matter for which he had called her.

"Carlotta, your virtuous attitude needs changing. You give out no news, either of marriage or divorce."

"I tell you again that I am very young for those things. Moreover, I have an unconquerable aversion to all men."

"Then you will have to have a wedding followed by a divorce."

"A marriage which is broken on leaving the church?"

"Yes, if necessary. The world is anxious for news. Your attitude irritates the public which goes to see our pictures."

Max York was chosen to be the groom in that imitation wedding. The news was sent broadcast over Europe, to be picked up by the antennae of the wireless systems.

It seemed as though the world held its breath and choked off its secret worries so that nothing might disturb that buoyant, laughing girl.

But there was nothing idyllic in the days before the wedding. Carlotta insisted that she hated no one so much as Max.

Elsa, furious at the news, finding her academy of kisses insufficient insult to her former lover, entered into open relations with Simpson. She kept him beside her as a shadow for her profile. She devoted herself to making him smile, so as to leave behind her and her automobile the flashing teeth of his negro laughter.

Two great stars cannot fall in love. They are governed by different laws, and each has a center of attraction which does not allow them to draw together. If they had said that Carlotta was going to marry a movie usher, the world would have believed in their future happiness, for a great star may take possession of a little one and hide it in her breast without having to break all the laws of the universe. But with Max there was certain failure.

Under the gaze of many cameras the wedding finally took place. The longest aisle in the world stretched before the bride and her attendants. The Movieland church was decorated with the most beautiful white lilies and the electric organ loosed all the angelic song birds on the air.

Every one was moved by a profound sadness mingled with deep envy. In the church where the ceremony was performed they seemed to be beneath the vaulted arches and under the lights of a great studio.

Carlotta, silent and disdainful, wore an exquisite gown of white tulle and carried a superb bouquet.

Max wore one of those marvelous jackets which gave him the air of a turtle dove. He carried his yellow gloves as though they were golden lilies.

The organ went on tossing notes out of its pipes like one of those trees of which one says, "I do not see how it can hold so many birds."

The bride and groom, on a cushion before the main altar, listened to the services.

The priest, tremulous before that woman, understood the irreparable wrong he was committing, the villainous act he was countenancing, the traitorous rôle he had played. He fled to the sacristy to fling himself down at a table and hide his head in his arms.

Every one was leaving the church as one leaves a place in which one must look out for the steppingstones, when a kind of dispute between Carlotta and Max attracted all the guests.

Max appeared to submit and the bride went with her friends back to her own hotel.

The blood suckers of the cinema clustered round her, fed off her, and followed after her, running on their tripods to the very bedroom in which she tore off her bridal veil. In her impatience she could not wait to take out the many pins which had held it.

CHAPTER XXXVIII

In the Elevator

Each day that passed, Carlotta offered herself as the most tempting figure on the screen of life. She needed neither manager nor promoter.

She was like an agile Amazon of love in the country of the movie cowboy who is skilled in throwing a lasso over a woman.

It was never possible to find her alone. She fled as though she were in a perpetual comedy of pursuit.

She was the spoiled darling of the world, of the entire solar system. That spoiling made her think only of how much she owed her anonymous public, until it became an offense for any one to approach her.

She had plenty of smiles for the magazine public, but none for an individual man.

She was a swimmer avoiding the nets which were set in the sea of Venus.

She went on repeating the mystery of innocence. She symbolized the young girl who comes out of the church scattering the perfume of her virginity.

She could not be a woman who has capitulated.

When one has yielded up one's body there is nothing more to charm or delight. One goes like a blind woman from fair to fair, blinded with the lights and the merry-go-rounds.

Carlotta wanted to be able to keep everything she saw within herself. She wanted depths within her heart. She could guard the sifted joy of life.

No one knew how it was accomplished, but the whole universe became new and exciting at the girl's least gesture. All men who saw her resented or forgot the women they had known before.

A single female flooded the widest strata of the rock of life with interest.

In the light of her charm everything was made charming. All manner of things gathered about her to form a background for her beauty.

She was like silken paper spread to hide all the defects and the failures of the world.

Vivid in everything she did, she painted her lips not with the affected air of a French girl, but as though her mouth had been struck by a voluptuous poignard, and the blow had made her lips bleed with sweetness and poison.

She carried the atmosphere of one whose career is predestined. It was as though she had been given Oriental powders, just as they give love potions to other girls.

She came near having her own little inn, but she still lived in the Movieland hotel, the hotel which had the most interesting hall in the world, for in that hall they tried out in real life things which would later be enacted in the imitation halls of the movies.

All possible snares were set in that foyer, but no one managed to get near Carlotta for more than a moment. It was as though no one was to be allowed beyond the reception room of her life.

The girl, who wanted to remain faithful to herself, chatted for a while in the hall, and if any one became too forward with insinuations she went straight to the elevator and was swallowed up by the brutal door that clashed its teeth behind her like jail bars.

The elevator boy stood at one side as they moved upward and watched her with the most abject devotion.

The elevator de luxe which went to the tenth floor where Carlotta lived—there were five more stories above her—was like the dressing room of a photographer's studio. A tiny boudoir table held combs and a hand mirror, hairpins and flasks of perfume.

The elevator boy, biting the chin strap of his cap, watched Carlotta as one might watch a landscape, or an unattainable being for whom one was merely the coachman.

The elevator boy did not dream that every one was in love with her. He believed himself to be one of the rashest mortals in the world.

Arriving at her floor, the boy opened the tiny door, and bade her a sad but disciplined farewell.

It was a poem of courtesy, set to the music of a submissive cornet. No one peered through the grating.

The elevator boy, grieved by the demands of people who wanted to go up, closed the heavy door and resigned himself to going down.

Carlotta loved that elevator. In it she was at peace. When they asked her if she liked to travel, she said, "Yes, in the elevator."

The elevator boy was like a student who went walking with his girl friend and embarked with her in the elevator. Sometimes he seemed her guardian angel, or a species of heavenly guide.

But behind his bashfulness, behind the mask of a reader of short stories, that trained and disciplined "buttons" cherished a silent passion for Carlotta.

He might be pardoned on the ground that it was impossible to be alone with that woman without trying to steal her sweet secrets.

So, one night the elevator boy who had never so much as raised his voice above a whisper, pushed the safety button to gain more time and threw himself on Carlotta.

It was inevitable that this should happen sometime to the elevator boy and the woman who ascends, and given Carlotta's rare beauty it was not strange that it should happen to her.

Carlotta, always prepared to defend herself, reached a hand over the clerkly embraces of the elevator boy and pressed the danger signal, which lit a red lamp in the office.

But the elevator boy, wanting to make the most of his moments, hugged Carlotta with the wide embrace of one who finds the task too much for him.

Carlotta, as though she were the organist of the elevator, pushed button after button, seeking the register of salvation.

Suddenly, as she touched one button, the diaphragm of her stomach tightened, and they went down as though they had been blasted by anathema itself.

The "buttons" who had counted on the factor of height, knew himself beaten, and began to cry like a child covered with the gilded buttons of a school boy.

Carlotta faced the weeping of a student caught at forbidden games, found the number of her floor on one of the round keys, and the elevator which had descended so rapidly went up once more like a balloon blown up with a fresh breath.

In the future she would mount the slow stairs. Never again would she enter a man's jail when man was inside.

She stepped out at her own floor with the grace of a trainer of wild horses. It was a pretty sight, but not one which would be repeated every day.

CHAPTER XXXIX

Lifena. The Cross-Eyed Man.
The Girl Whom Nobody Loved. The Psychoanalyst.
The Jewish Quarter. Details.

THAT BEAUTIFUL WOMAN who had appeared in Movieland with the sweet name of Lifena seemed to want to comfort the inhabitants for Carlotta's cruel indifference.

Her mission was exactly contrary to Carlotta's. She was the comforter. She cured the fevers which Carlotta provoked as though she had been a Red Cross mission dedicated to love. Lifena had five different beds in five bedrooms, each of a different style.

It was one of the charms of that houseful of doors and corridors that they opened on rooms which were the ante-chambers of other rooms.

"I do not see how one can have only one couch and one bedroom. That is a monstrosity that could be conceived only by married couples who prefer depravity to a certain appearance of indecency. And there is such a vast difference between depravity and indecency!"

Lifena's theory was that an ordinary lonely bedroom, full of boredom and frustration, of commonplace dreams and half suppressed sighs, was no place in which to spend a happy night. So, she had a bedroom which was serious and another which was gay, a frivolous one, and one which was draped in mourning, and she used whichever was best suited to the person she was receiving.

One of her bedrooms was locked, and only "the traveler" who came to Movieland once every six or seven months, had the key to it. No one else ever shared that bedroom with her. And he was as contented as though that were the greatest favor he could ask.

Like every great film city, Movieland had its cross-eyed man. A comic type, he was funny for reasons that lay outside himself and were visible only to the eyes that looked at him. No astigmatic realizes that being cross-eyed is funny only to other people. A man who is born that way can take advantage of it and can exaggerate his clowning secure in the knowledge that the thing which lies in his eyes and which is too sad for laughter is the very thing at which other people laugh.

The cross-eyed man changed all Movieland's way of looking at things. He made every one a trifle cross-eyed.

One of his eyes peered toward his nose, the other wandered sidewise as though it were looking for a thread on the shoulder of his coat.

From the bottom of his wall-eyed soul, Audrey fell in love with Carlotta, like all the rest of them. His sadness produced a phenomenon in his wry eyes which made them all the funnier.

There is a current belief that one should be very formal with cross-eyed folk and should have due sympathy with their defect. But so far as the great clown of the cross-eyes was concerned, people paid no attention to the theory. He awoke the most crazy mirth, mirth which in itself was cross-eyed.

As he himself said, "There are plenty of girls like these, round and fresh, with hair that curls into gay ringlets. But there is only one cross-eyed man like me in the world. It would be very difficult to find my equal."

Another novel sight in Movieland was a submissive and ingenuous young person who all her life had been the girl that nobody loves. The personality of this girl on whom no lover ever called had a great success in the films.

She had a manager worthy of the name, for without him no one would ever have dreamed that that girl, with her pale hair, could ever be anything but a school girl just out of the convent, limp as a duck, clumsy as an awkward child.

Just as in old time revolutionary meetings they were always crying the warning, "There is a government agent among us," so in Movieland they were constantly on guard against a psychoanalyst.

Law-abiding folk feared him as though he were a disturber of the peace. They were as much afraid of him as they would have been of a spy, and they searched for him among the tourist throng as they would have hunted a traitor.

The main studio of Dr. Playel was the place where he analyzed the principal exponents of the movie art, and established to his own satisfaction the class of criminals to which they belonged, or the category in which they would have lived had they stayed in the world and devoted themselves to one of the professions.

The case history of each person held an amusing list of possibilities assigned to him. They were as good as short stories.

To him the faces of all the great screen stars were faces of criminals—inmates of Sing Sing. Any one of those men would scare people in real life and would have been thrown out of high society as typical adventurers.

One of Dr. Playel's psychoanalytic tests was to put a grating in front of each screen star's face and see what he looked like behind the bars. Almost all of them looked like confirmed highwaymen.

Dr. Playel hid himself in the rôle of a character actor playing the part of an astronomer in "The Vision of Mars." He concealed his personality, but he took many notes and wrote long comments in his hotel. His pen fairly leaped out of the inkwell in his anxiety to note down observations and more observations.

The Jewish quarter of Movieland grows more powerful every day. It is almost as though the great imitation city were the land which was promised but never won. Perhaps in a town of such modern type the ancient stigma may be lost and the unattainable be realized. Perhaps Movieland may triumph over the dissension aroused by any mention of the return to Jerusalem.

The life of the Jewish quarter is a thing of the most gorgeous exuberance. Beautiful pale women look down from its balconies, women who bear the ill-will of all femininity.

The race that was sent wandering by divine command will finally set up its tents in Movieland. It will stay for a long time, as though it were in a cemetery of the living.

The beautiful Jewess, flower of that fairy-tale city, is mistress of a level stare which some day will conquer all the frail and slender stars.

Only with such compelling deceit as built that beautiful city can they fool God and persuade him to let them return.

Over the movie city there hangs that curse which threatened Jerusalem: "There shall not be left here one stone upon another that shall not be thrown down."

They always seem to be listening for heavenly words which will prophesy the end of Movieland.

Therefore, the Jews live in Movieland as in an ideal town always half devastated and ready to end the whole thing every evening, although they take advantage of the interval to do very well by themselves.

No false whiskers. The movie actor who must wear a beard grows one.

"How long does it take to grow a beard for the part of

Landru?"

"From six to eight and a half months."

But the most usual thing is a half grown beard, weedy and a bit moth-eaten.

Careton the Magnificent decided one day to announce in all the European newspapers that he wanted to get married. He received an appalling number of answers. "The earth is so full of people that it scares one to think of them," he declared. Almost all the replies ran like this:

> "My dear Careton:
>
> My husband does not understand me. He will not buy me new clothes, he does not want me to wear chiffon stockings, though, as you can see by the enclosed photograph, I am very beautiful. I want to leave him and join you there. How much does the trip cost?"

One of those geniuses that Movieland shelters is inventing a new advertising stunt. He will group the stars of the Milky Way into a high-powered sign so arranged that it will inscribe the name of the success across the face of the entire sky.

Josue, who is Movieland's most famous clown, has a farm on which he breeds ducks and nothing else. Ducks come and go through all the rooms of his farmhouse.

"They are the predecessors of Charlie Chaplin and of all the silent humor of the screen," he used to tell people who came to visit him.

Josue contends that any one who lives in the midst of a flock of ducks is bound to stay young.

But lately he has grown very sad, and returned into the inmost depths of his duck domicile. In the middle of one of his funniest films a movie fan died of laughter.

They think it is possible to make a world of simpletons, devoid of any distinguishing characteristic except their type.

The limit of originality will be the smoking of a pipe and the filling of the atmosphere with the banal odor of specially grown tobacco.

The hours of their lives are those which are marked on the vacuous white faces of bathroom clocks.

CHAPTER XL

The Man With the Muddy Face

THE HUGE WHITE AUTOMOBILE whirled into the city. It was apparent that the man who came flying in this mad fashion was its owner, as he carried an air of seeing nobody. He was as thickly coated with mud as the rest of them. It made a kind of mask for his face, specked with dried pellets and lumpy with bits of clay.

Dressed in mud, he leaped out of the huge car the moment it reached the plaza, and asked for Carlotta Bray. They guided him to the little house with its neat awnings. In a moment he was pulling up before the door of the most fascinating girl in the world. She looked out of the window to see who was coming.

The man with the muddy face, whose outside coating was dotted with bits of gravel, leaped to the ground. Enveloped in a helmet more proper to an aviator than to a motorist, his features obscured by the mask of clay he had collected on his journey, he knocked at the door with all the assurance of a medieval warrior clad in irons.

Carlotta looked dubiously down at him from her balcony and asked, "For whom are you looking?"

"For Carlotta Bray," the muddy man answered, and then, recognizing her, corrected himself, "For you."

Carlotta did not know what to answer, but she distrusted that man who bore the tangible record of great distances.

"And what do you want of me?"

The man who looked as though he had fallen out of the muddy craters of the moon was disconcerted.

"I have driven five hundred miles at top speed for the sole purpose of being able to converse with the woman who moves the entire world. I am a son of Worfeller the millionaire."

Carlotta, taking no account of the daring which had turned that man into something resembling a slimy toad, answered as she closed the window, "Then you may drive five hundred miles back again, for I shall not receive you." And Carlotta shut the balcony doors.

All his millions were thrown back in young Worfeller's face, and even the mud which covered it grew pink with his blushes.

Yet, having speeded through the tunnel of distance which had begun in the rose colored movie palace and ended in Movieland, he could not bear to go back empty-handed.

The white automobile was jumping as though it had St. Vitus' dance. Even with the brake on it was making imaginary flights that convulsed its backbone with the illusion of speed.

That pale girl whom he had thought to conquer instantly had shut herself up in a house of frail glass which he dared not break.

The young millionaire, looking like a savage in his coat of mud, took out his check book, and marking off ciphers with a fountain pen especially made for that purpose, wrote two checks for enormous sums, signed them, and scribbled a most urgent note on the back of them.

The vulnerable part of a house is that slot in the door marked "LETTERS." He dropped his two checks face downward through the slot. Then he rang the bell. A voice answered, and Worfeller begged:

"Have Miss Carlotta read the letter I dropped in her box."

There was a moment of silence. The car waited; the muddy man was poised as though they were going to open the garage door for him.

A movie maid in the smart cap of a well-trained servant came out with a tray, and on it, in little pieces as though arranged for a game of drawing numbers, were the two torn checks.

With a furious gesture of balked pride, the masked man wiped off a handful of the mud that hid his features, and flung it at the middle window. Then he leaped into his car and tore away.

There were two sharp explosions as though his tires had burst, and in Carlotta's windows two holes like tiny eyes appeared.

CHAPTER XLI

Russian Princesses. The Man on the Bridge.
He Who Looks Like Ravarol.
The King They Seek. Make-Believe Sailors.

HOW WAS IT THAT so many Russian princesses came to Movieland! They were as smoothly pale as cold cream, and they did not know how to behave. In the pictures they were querulous and sad.

Other women who never had been princesses wore a queen's crown with all the dignity of monarchs entering on a long reign. A queen must be gay, and the exiled princesses, worn out with loneliness and melancholy, were cast as ragged servants or pathetic dress makers.

The head of the Movieland employment office, who hunted all over the world for types, brought back from his travels a fine haul of the type that is known as "the man on the bridge."

Men on bridges are special beings who give the sense of real life to a film. They lean on the bridge railing watching the currents flow past them, and speculating on the broad and mysterious stream of life. Men come and go, but they are immovable as the bridge piers. No one not of their type can imitate them. They arouse all the emotion of a Ponson du Terrail.

How lucky he was! He was leaning on a bridge when a stranger came up and stood beside him, watching the waters which ran by him, and casting a glance at the idlers. The stranger had been on other bridges watching other men, but he had chosen none of them.

He stayed beside this man for an hour, and then asked:

"How would you like to come to Movieland at a good salary and do nothing but go on gazing from bridges, or maybe sitting on benches at the curve of a road and watching the automobiles whirl past?"

The man thought he was making fun of him. He had never suspected that in his very idleness he was preparing himself for a well-paid profession.

The famous murderer Ravarol, whose crimes made those of other famous criminals seem like the tricks of children, brought good fortune to a man who looked like him, and who became a leading movie star solely because of that resemblance.

The employment agent had had great difficulty in finding an actor who could double for the crook with the invisible eyes.

A specialist in faces, he hunted the highways and the byways, the city squares and the bar rooms for a man who looked enough like the famous criminal so that his picture might thrill the whole world.

In a tiny Brussels café he found one of those men who watch the street in the bottom of a wine glass as though they were looking at it through a bottle. "Ravarol," he exclaimed.

After that first picture, the supposed Ravarol lived in Movieland like a criminal who had escaped from the guillotine, telling the story of his crimes to any one who would listen.

But the thing that most amused Movieland, which had a smile for everything, was the sudden news that a real king, with a real crown and everything, a reigning king, had taken refuge in the midst of its hosts.

Every one wondered who the king was, and each asked the other in fun if he were king. Undoubtedly the question came at one time or the other to the ears of the hidden king himself.

Could the king, characterized as a great movie star, be one of those bearded men whose original face not God himself could recognize?

Diplomatic notes came, and special police. Intimate friends of the king came to see if they could find him.

No one knew where he was. There were so many people there without rôles that there was no way of locating him.

But the king was undoubtedly there, for letters from him were received from time to time in his own land.

That king whom none could find, a king with real power, a king for whom his people clamored, was one of the pet mysteries of Movieland.

What attitude would the king take in a cabaret, how would he look lost in the mob of soldiery that surrounded other kings?

At last he was free from that absurd world which sets up goals no man can reach. At last he was in a world without any sense, an inexplicable world, sustained by an imitation of the real world which is all one huge joke.

That world proposed nothing, neither law nor art nor welfare.

It was a huge and eccentric world, unjustifiable, impossible of belief. There were about it the conditions of verisimilitude, yet its truths were never proved.

The most one can achieve in this world is that absurdity which is without pretense. The king who had escaped the whole burden of life outside was there where everything had the capricious air of chance and individual luck.

The imitation naval officers of Movieland went dancing up and down in their white trousers like jumping jacks pulled by a string.

Happy sailors always in port, they grew as serious in the kissing hour as though they were giving kisses in the livid light of a shipwreck.

Make-believe sailors of make-believe voyages, their sweethearts believed they had just landed and were about to sail away at once, so they flung themselves passionately on their gold-buttoned breasts.

Side-whiskered and pale, they smoked cigarettes in long holders with an air of boasting that they had sailed all the seas and had left sweethearts in every port.

There are in Movieland certain formidable old men with bearded smiles who meet in the Senators' bar. People who see them think them an international congress of prime ministers.

They smoke endless stogies, and everything infuriates them, but they always have hopes of fixing things up and they always do. Devoted to the films, they play the part of fathers who plant the most incestuous of kisses on the cheeks of their amazing daughters.

The great boxers one sees are not the real ones. They are men who look like the real ones, men brutal and debased who have twisted noses and cauliflower ears.

Movie actors never wear the same necktie twice. They would be out-moded if they disobeyed this physico-moral law for a single day. Those artists of the seventh art have no right to a neck cloth.

Movieland is also full of fake financiers. They are those young men in English clothes who look everything up and down as if they were going to buy it, or as if they were about to sign a check for the whole business.

CHAPTER XLII

Carlos Wilh Tries to Rape Carlotta Bray.
The Rape and Death of Carlotta Bray.

As time passed Carlotta Bray became more opulent. She was one of those adolescent Carlottas (her age was seventeen and a half) who are half-women and half-children, whose legs shake like their cheeks—Carlottas that later will become like parrots for coarse hair will sprout from their beauty spots. . . .

Carlotta Bray was, above all, the free woman—the woman who lives alone and who can open her windows whenever she damn pleases.

She was, decidedly, the most tempting star, the star of the hour. In the films Carlotta always came out chastely like the ideal fiancée, and this chastity was responsible for her many wonderful successes.

The passions of all Movieland burned hot about her. She knew so well how to make people love her!

More than anything else she inflamed her public with that pet gesture of hers—the gesture with which she put on a pearl necklace.

In almost all the films there was that gesture of receiving the necklace with delicate modesty when the clasp finally chained it about her neck.

It might almost have been called the sacrament of the pearls. Its ritual had all the solemnity of baptism.

When it was her lover who clasped the pearls about her neck she blushed as though she were receiving her first kiss. As he snapped the catch she accepted his kiss as though a diamond pendant fallen close on her throat had struck her through with a divine shiver.

When it was the old man she hated, but had accepted because of his wealth, she became a great actress. Under the hands that clasped the necklace she was indifferent, resigned, ashamed, and when the old man asked a smile of gratitude her gesture was a study in cloaked disdain.

"That is Carlotta Bray's house," the rest of them—the movie bandit, the gypsy who did her Sunday dancing in the streets every day—said as they passed the cottage.

The house was white and hung with red geraniums which dripped from green boxes that edged every window.

One Sunday—this was a true Sunday, and not one of the six others that were imitations—the famous Carlos Wilh felt in the mood of a thief and a criminal. His whole being was charged with bottled-up energy, and he felt the need of spending it on something extraordinary.

"Sitting on a café terrace on Sunday is almost as bad as committing suicide," he said. Moved by some secret impulse he walked toward Carlotta's house, eager to drink of something as potent as one of those strange and precious liquors which lie hidden in the farthest corners of cellars.

He found several of Carlotta's friends adoring that gay and ravishing queen of curves.

Wilh was as ridiculous as a great fat babe in arms. On seeing him enter, the superproducer Gans crossed one leg over the other with infinite weariness. The creator of *Fireworks* wore socks meant to dazzle the eye of the beholder, and a pair of those shoes which are pure rhythm wrought in leather. Each line and curve is thought out with such care that they become the perfect embodiment of the pedestrian soul.

The drug fiend, Girys, who always plays a villain's rôle, hovered in Gans' shadow. He was one of those malignant men whose words, seeming to be the fruit of measured reflection, left a bitter sting behind them. Racked by disease, both lungs shot full of holes, he was evil where other men were good. He was bored by everything, he had a kind of low disdain for everything which was clear cut and definite.

Wise students of mankind despised him, although his voice had a certain mellifluous quality, and the most deceitful ingenuousness in the world.

Slim, over-bearing, his eyes too bright, there was something of the spider in him.

The flattery in his smile, and a gleam of adulation which played about his cancerous lips, won him invitations to all the parties. When he laughed it was as though he were flat on his back in a field, his feet waving in the air like an overturned beetle.

Dr. Erbert, the actor who always played the doctor's rôle in pictures, completed the group.

"Shall we improvise a grand supper party?" asked the fat Wilh.

"Yes. A noisy supper party which will turn Sunday upside down." The youth with a head like a hammer was more definite.

"All the women to the kitchen," ordered the superproducer.

Everything was organized with instant efficiency. Every one went to his own house to get some special dish. The table became a luxurious beach on the fertile coast of the old tropics. They even achieved a jazzband, which gave the dining-room the air of a ship in torment. The diners increased the din by adding the noises of clashing plates to the sharp notes of the jazzband.

Carlotta, always in character, lost none of her serenity, though the other women had begun to welcome the hot hands of the men on their cool shoulders.

Carlotta always said disdainfully, "Love is as repugnant to

me as are uncooked snails to any one who does not like them. If one could only wash lovers in a series of waters and then cook them! But they are so raw and crude they make me ill."

Carlotta was radiant, standing tall and erect in a robe held only by a single pin clasped on her left hip. It looked as though one flashing turn on her toes would fling it open and disclose the statue hidden among her draperies.

They talked of Max.

"He is one of those," Carlotta said, "who ask eternal love in return for a box of candy."

Then they snarled themselves up in a moving picture conversation.

"We never get applause. They clap at the sheets on which we appear as Christ appeared on Veronica's handkerchief."

"But on the other hand we never hear the hissing, nor have our eyes blinded by the rotten eggs they throw at the screen when they don't like the picture. Believe me, silence and absence are a good deal better."

"Our souls are filtered through too many processes."

"And our projection is monotonous. If I had a son I would forbid his going into the movies."

"I have already told mine he couldn't."

They had reached dessert.

"Fruit seems slimy as a snake to me. I want sweets," cried Carlotta.

Carlos Wilh, a bit drunk, went back to talking of love.

"Let them give us a moment of pleasure as long as eternity, as long as though they had never left us, as long as though they were never going to leave us."

He raised his cup like an orator clearing the decks for action.

Carlos Wilh looked at Carlotta like one of those pointers with elephant's skin and a pair of white eyes set in the middle of a sooty face. He was growing redder and redder, and his short neck rose above his collar like a bloody muffler.

Every one had drunk a bit too much. They began to dance. Couple after couple disappeared into other rooms and then came back again.

The jazzband pressed its notes harder and harder.

Carlos Wilh danced on and on with Carlotta. From time to time he slowed his steps, and plunging his rumpled head into a cup, he washed himself down with champagne.

For a long time the other dancers saw nothing of him.

Suddenly Elena's scream rose high above the noise of the jazzband, Georgiana begged piteously: "A doctor! A doctor!"

There was Doctor Erbert, the finest type of movie doctor in the world. Livid, useless, his eyes blurred by wine till they looked like splotches of ink which run when water falls on them, he did not dare to interfere.

Atalanta, for the moment unconscious of her beauty, clad only in the light tunic of a bathing suit, implored him with her eyes.

Impelled by the duty he owed the films, Erbert moved toward the room of the accident. Every one stepped aside to let the imitation doctor pass. Even in the midst of his intoxication and the sudden evidence of unexpected reality, he felt himself a doctor bound to do his best in a film tragedy.

The girl who was as perfect as a dream could not be really dead. Those arms of hers could not have died, unless it was for the immortality bestowed by a museum on its choicest marbles.

Erbert, like every one else, raised her head and tried to awaken her from what must surely be pretense. Her arms flung wide and inert, she seemed a swimmer floating on the tide of death.

Her dead arms had not fallen into angles like those of fainting women in the films. Carlotta's arms fell straight and rigid, dead pendulums of tragedy. The watch on her dead wrist ticked on like a ghost, like a pulse where the blood would never beat again.

That fallen arm, sounding the very depths of death, was the thing that proved her dead beyond the shadow of a doubt.

CHAPTER XLIII

Death on the Screen

After that scandal went echoing through the world, the metropolis ordered Movieland, the new Sodom and Gomorrah, closed.

The death of the world's sweetheart justified the shutting down of this free and modern town. It had failed every one, and it had let that flashing virginity escape from every one.

Carlotta's films were shown over and over again in all the movie houses of the world. Pantheons of the dead, they were full of brothers and sisters who could not be persuaded to go anywhere together except to the movies.

Many sisters, looking as though they had just shaved their necks and were afraid of taking cold in them, gathered in front of the flaming billboards to stare at Carlotta in all her wild purity.

The finest thing about the movies—their free recognition of passion, their enormous native vigor, their revolt against the absurdities of the world within the borders of Movieland—was absent from that film, for every one knew that the great city was closed and its life dead.

The voice of the entire audience greeted Carlotta when she appeared on the great white sheet which was her shroud.

There was more sadism in that nightly triumph of the dead girl than in the violent scene which had caused her death. To sit face to face with a ghost whose body lay buried and rotting in the grave was to feel in one's inmost soul the passion of death. And when the dead girl appeared with her lovely form veiled lightly in filmy lingerie—

Her shoulders were never reconciled to death. With all the strength of their beautiful curves they denied that they had died.

Everything emphasized the crime of the fat man who appeared on the screen with her, girded about with a great belt punctured with astonished eyelets.

He hugged her to the point of strangulation with force stored up in many mornings of sport and play, and the crowd hooted at him.

Many times the film had to be recut in the projection rooms when it reached those scenes with Wilh in which she was, as it were, cremated without losing either form or life.

All her smiles were haunted with a sense of farewell, and it became evident that even when she played hardest she had a presentiment of what was going to happen.

The paradox of life is more vivid than even in the movement and the action of films of the dead. That which was unforgettable in the past comes back to life along with the people.

The feeling that "he might almost be alive" makes the son weep when he sees his father in the movies. He would look just like that in real life, with the same gestures, and the same joy of living that pulses through all gestures, even when they are those of weeping.

If tearful cries greeted the appearance of a beloved father, Carlotta's appearance evoked sobs and an anguish which wrung all the tear ducts.

Found with this memory of the living, the paradox of ceasing to live in an instant short as the winking of an eye becomes even more absurd.

One did not cease to live, nor cease to be born, nor cease to have died. Consolation lies in the undeniable fact of having been here, a memory which always beats anew, and if this be too little, there is that cinematographic proof which contradicts the whole falsehood called absence and death.

The projecting machine sounded as loud in the silence as a clock which overpowers all who listen to it.

Carlotta was already becoming a bit démodé. Things out of fashion in the movies do not stay conveniently dead as they do in magazines and photographs. They go on living, they justify themselves, one even sees that once upon a time they might have aroused enthusiasm.

The thing one notices is that the masquerade of life, from that point of view, is always a masquerade. At the time, it seems important to fools, but it never is.

Carlotta put on her pearl necklaces with the same gesture—a bit démodé now—as when she first took them glowing from their case.

Yet the light that slid caressingly over those pearls was a bit different, as becomes the fading light of the past. When that keepsake was young it lived in light like a throbbing tremulous gland.

But the picture which awoke the most emotion was the one played in the old castle, the castle of all our fairy tales. On its tallest tower sat two old owls which blink their eyes at the night in a wink which expressed all we know about death, all we have known since the stone age.

Those movie chimes which are heard rather by the heart than the ear, swung their iron clappers with the slow, heavy tolling that follows after death.

Usually they seem to ring across the fields from a distant hill but in the dead girl's picture they were like a whisper of death come to disturb a holiday.

Running backward over that life, one found a strange seriousness, and everything seemed to watch as the conspiracy gathered about Carlotta.

Every one took comfort in the faint perfume of Carlotta that remained. Her life had been so premature that a whole great city must be closed to atone for its taking.

But what could they know of that life which was the more irrevocably dead because it could not renew itself in the producing of new films?

Nothing. Everything was guesswork, and those who knew it best were the ushers in blue uniforms, anxious to shut up the cashier's cage of the empty theater. A theater without actors for greater economy sometimes utilizes the very shadows of the dead.

And on the empty movie billboards that had flaunted the flaming ads of the dead girl's films there hung the sable robe of night.

THE END

ACKNOWLEDGMENTS

Profound thanks are extended to the following for their generous financial support which helped to defray some of this book's production costs:

Alan J Abrams, Jamey Adirim, Zynab Hashim Al-Ma'Ali,
John Alvey, Matthew Armsworth, Stiarna Askew,
Diana Baldovino, Thomas Young Barmore Jr, Nick Barry,
Doug Bedwell, Traci Belanger, Kian S. Bergstrom, Sam Bertram,
Brad Bigelow (The Neglected Books Page), Brian R. Boisvert,
BR, David Brownless, Giancarlo Cairella, Chris Call,
Noah Castellanos, Sebastian Castillo, Scott Chiddister,
Chelsea Clifton, Joel Coblentz, Jason Crane,
Malcolm & Parker Curtis, Robert Dallas, AJ Danna,
William P Davis, dcMalone,
Diana Mourey DeFisher for Larry Ann Evans, Daniel M Dion,
Dylan & Sam Doomwarre, Daniel Dorman, Boaz David Dror,
Alfred Eaker, David Edmonds, Curtis B. Edmundson,
Isaac Ehrlich, Ricky Engelhardt, Richard Faught, Randy Fields,
Frederick Filios, Ken Finlayson, George Denley Fischer,
Andrew Fisher, Mark Flemmich, Anthony Fletcher,
Dennis Forsgren, Thomas Fuchs, Stephen Fuller, Justin Gallant,
John M. Gamble, Pierino Gattei, Stephan Glander, GMarkC,
Sam Goldstein, David Greenberg, Richard L. Haas III,
Lisa Hagerman, Aaron Hanson, Mahan Harirsaz,
Heather Haskins, Haya, Aric Herzog, Wesley Hoffman,
Fred W Johnson, Alex Juarez, Jennifer Keenan, Nathan Kouri,
Kyle, Mark Lamb, J. A. Lee, Rick Lewis, Peyton Light,

Gardner Linn, Nick Long, William Lorenzo,
Fester L.D. MacKrell, Mike Mancini, Jim McElroy,
Conall McGarrigle, Donald McGowan,
Dr. Melvin "Steve" Mesophagus, Jason H Miller, mky,
Gardner Monks, Spencer F Montgomery, Moog, Steven Moore,
Geoffrey Moses, Gregory Moses, Luke Mosher,
Scott Murphy, Clyde Nads, April A. Nielsen,
Michael O'Shaughnessy, Nick Oxford, Andrew Pearson,
Andrew Pizzey, Pedro Ponce, Stephen Press,
Nicholas Grendel Rabinowicz, Ned Raggett, David Raposa,
Judith Redding, Oliver S,
George Salis (www.TheCollidescope.com), Don Schulz,
Scott Seago, Serpent Moon, Jonathan Sieders,
Alexander Silva-Sadder, Jason Smith, Yvonne Solomon,
Jared Stearns, Martin E Stein & Scott A Saxon, K. L. Stokes,
S. Taush, Tim Tucker, Sydney Umana, Dan Visel,
Ashley Walker, G. David Wells, C Wendland,
Christopher Wheeling, Isaiah Whisner, Charlie Wilcox,
Charles Wilkins, Jeff Wilson, Chris Wolf, T.R. Wolfe,
The Zemenides Family, and Anonymous

www.ingramcontent.com/pod-product-compliance
Ingram Content Group UK Ltd.
Pitfield, Milton Keynes, MK11 3LW, UK
UKHW012247290726
14090UKWH00013B/520